Nov 22, 2015

Chief Lehncker,

To a cop's cop!

My very best personal regards,

Joe

FREDONIA

A Sgt. James Kilbane Story

By

JOSEPH J. FITZGERALD

Copyright © 2010 by Joseph J. Fitzgerald

ISBN 0-7414-5883-7

Printed in the United States of America

This is a work of fiction. Names, characters, places, and incidents either are the product of the author's imagination or are used fictitiously. Any resemblance to actual events or locales or persons, living or dead, is entirely coincidental.

Published May 2010

INFINITY PUBLISHING
1094 New DeHaven Street, Suite 100
West Conshohocken, PA 19428-2713
Toll-free (877) BUY BOOK
Local Phone (610) 941-9999
Fax (610) 941-9959
Info@buybooksontheweb.com
www.buybooksontheweb.com

DEDICATION

This book is dedicated to the memory of

LOUIS J. DEREUIL

A real hero and a true friend

ACKNOWLEDGMENTS

The author gratefully acknowledges the gracious assistance of Ms. Kelly Hilding of the Town of Fredonia, and Ms. Maureen Tait of the Fredonia-Kanab Historical Society for taking me into the magic of the sister cities.

Also Deputy Jason Bundy, of the Coconino County Sheriff's Office, for his insight into the cooperation of the law enforcement agencies in that corner of the world.

And finally Robert Perkins, a Fort Lauderdale private investigator, who was an immense help in bringing me up to date on the latest technologies.

THE COVER

When you looked at the cover you may have seen the haunting face of the killer lurking just left of the trees.

The cover was created by one of the author's sons who designs web sites and commercial advertisements.

JOSEPH S. FITZGERALD

AT

JOELUCKY39 @ .COM

PROLOGUE

My father, Mike Kilbane, was a cop who, for many years, pounded a beat in the theater district of downtown Boston. In the fall of 1983 he responded to a burglar alarm at a jewelry store where false alarms were too much of a habit. He arrived to find Mr. and Mrs. Levine standing together behind the counter and two men in business suits seated, their attention drawn to a tray of diamonds. The owners, with a signal that everything was all right, offered the usual apologetic smiles and my father turned to leave.

It suddenly struck him that there was something wrong with the picture. For one thing both customers were male! For another, the smiles of the couple, well known to him, seemed a trifle forced!

My father should have kept going but instead he stopped to turn back. The Levine's bolted for the back room and my father was gunned down.

A few days later, on the front steps of St. Paul's while the bagpipes were still playing, my mother took my brother and me, each by the hand, and made us make a solemn promise never to become police officers.

Today my brother, Mike, coaches football at the college level and I am a homicide detective with the Broward County Sheriff's Office in Florida.

CHAPTER ONE

On a Saturday in mid-October a pretty Florida girl had gone to the beach and vanished. A few hours later her purple Corvette was found sitting on a sabotaged flat tire. That is why, on a sun-lit Sunday, when I was supposed to be playing golf, I was, instead, climbing the stairs to the wrap-around deck of a town house in the well-heeled town of Hillsboro.

The brightly colored town houses overlooking the Intra-Coastal Waterway had more of a New England look about them and were about as cozy as a couple of million dollars could manage. Given the extravagance of the surrounding area, the failed attempt at understatement seemed eminently suited to what I had recently learned of Stoddard Lee.

Lee was a former football star at Penn State, a first round draft choice of the Miami Dolphins and one of the bigger busts in the history of the NFL. But his timing away from the gridiron couldn't have been better. About the time it was discovered that his size fourteens weren't quick enough to cut off the outside rush, the cellular telephone was just coming of age. So Lee, with a classmate's persuasion, invested his considerable signing bonus in a company that was building radio towers and the rest is history. Today he could buy the Dolphins on his own if he were so disposed or unbothered by the bitter memories of his all-too brief professional football experience.

The odd thing is that, for a former jock, Stoddard Lee would have to be considered a near introvert. He made a point of avoiding his former football associates, too many of whom, at least in his mind, were in a hurry to go broke or looking for some kind of help. Lee's one indulgence was beautiful women and too often to suit him his picture would crop up in the local magazines and newspapers with some well-adorned beauty on his arm. His playing the field came to an end, however, when, in his later forties, he hooked up with the exceptionally beautiful, Caroline Albright.

The multi-colored medley of town houses with the name of Pelican's Cove were built by Stoddard Lee and sold for a premium in the weeks before the slump. The homes consisted of two levels above four car garages with wood stairways that led to wood decks. Lee's unit on the north end of the complex afforded the broader view.

I completed my climb to the deck and before my finger caught the doorbell I was treated to the tile scratching charge of a formidable dog with a bark loud enough to separate any ordinary visitor from his shoes.

"Hush, Bear!" a female voice said sharply. "You quiet down this minute!" And, on cue, there was an immediate, near miraculous silence.

The ponderous door swung open with the confidence gained in having a 120-pound co-host. Beginning at the ankles and on up to the knees, the irrepressible Rottie made a methodical evaluation of me with more curiosity, I wanted to believe, than suspicion!

"Yes, Sergeant," the white flannel clad matron said, taking my card. "Mr. Lee is expecting you. He has been on the phone all morning and is just now getting out of the shower." There was a time-modified lilt of the old country in her voice.

With Bear's nose planted in the back of one knee we trooped down a narrow hall and into the "Great Room", a spacious expanse beneath a cathedral ceiling with an entire wall of glass that looked down on the tributary below.

Inside there was an informal scattering of sofas and chairs, a sizeable bar, a weight bench and a 60" television screen, currently quiet. I calculated the weights to be an intimidating 450 pounds, again consistent with the little I had come to know of Stoddard Lee. An iron spiral stairway led to an L-shaped catwalk balcony that fronted the upstairs bedrooms, four in all counting the knobs. There was a wall at the far end of the room with alcoves that led to the partially visible kitchen and dining room.

The bar was situated against the wall farthest from the windows and off to the side was another door that suggested still another bedroom, office or den. Or perhaps all three! Above the bar was one of those large photographs that had been airbrushed into what looked like an original painting. It was obviously of our missing girl and she was every bit as breathtaking as the scouting report claimed. Blonde, green-eyed, and poured into a pale blue gown, she was half turned away and looking back over a strapless shoulder.

"Can I get you some coffee, Sergeant? Mr. Lee is going to be a few minutes at least."

"Thank you," I said, sliding onto one of the stools. "Cream and no sugar if you don't mind!"

Bear was making an improbable effort to burrow into the tile while watching me intently, his head and eyes so large that it was like looking at the screen from the front row of a movie theater. But my attention was, unavoidably, diverted to the beauty above the bar.

It was Sunday, normally my day off! But just as I was tossing my golf clubs into the back of my Honda, Captain Abrams, in keeping with his continued effort to send my handicap soaring, nailed me on the cell phone once again. So it was back into the house where I ran off the missing person report on the computer and changed into a suit. And by midmorning I was climbing the stairs at Pelican's Cove

"This came straight from the sheriff," Abrams had told me. "He wants you on this case and no one else! I don't know if you know who Stoddard Lee is but he is, according to Fortune Magazine, one of the fifty wealthiest in South Florida as well as a historic bust at pro football! Every time the subject of notable busts comes up his name is sure to be included!"

My eyes were still fixed on the beauty above the bar when the housekeeper returned with my coffee.

"That's Caroline!" the maid said quietly, putting the mug on the bar. "Beautiful, isn't she?" I had been so absorbed in my thoughts I hadn't heard her coming.

"And she is every bit as lovely a person as she is beautiful! Both Mr. Lee and I have given up hope of ever seeing her again! What's the point of kidding ourselves! Something terrible has happened to her and we both know it. With her car found sitting on a flat tire and all. It's over! I know it!" Her blue Irish eyes were brimming.

Well I wouldn't give up just yet!" I said. "I've seen a lot of victims survive kidnappings before. And there are a lot of other possible explanations!"

"I'm Margaret, by the way," she said, looking at me doubtfully. "And poor Bear, here. I don't know what will happen to him. This was her dog entirely and I've seen dogs die of broken hearts before."

The dog's big brown eyes, still fixed on me, quite eerily seemed to know! It was as though he was pleading with me to make things right!

The door at the far end finally swung open and the hulking form of Stoddard Lee came into view. He gave a nod

6

and a half smile to Margaret as she padded off toward the kitchen while he strode to the bar. He was wearing a gray sweatshirt and jeans, as well as the only thing about him that suggested real money; deck shoes with no socks. His short blonde hair was matted from his recent shower and he was large enough to warrant his own zip code! Not that he had a lot of muscle definition, really, and his abs had probably given out some years before. He was just beefy big. He looked like the kind of guy whose daily exercise regimen was to bench the poundage across the room and call it a day. His craggy good looks were even craggier from his night without sleep.

"Detective Sergeant James P. Kilbane," he read from the card as he took a stool twice removed from me, "Why do I know that name!"

"I've been around a while," I said, without any intention of helping him there.

"I appreciate the department's response. It's been all I could ask. I know with missing adults you don't normally begin to investigate for a couple of days! I heard all about that last night! But everyone's been great. Officer Hanstein could have left it to me to check the hospitals last night but instead she sat with me and we split the calls."

Margaret was back with his coffee and took a stool at the far end of the bar, which probably said a lot about the level of trust between them.

"Have you seen the report?" he asked.

"I took it off the computer this morning."

"Have they determined yet if the tire on her car had been deliberately punctured?"

"With an awl or an ice pick. There was no impediment

7

found in the tire!" It was not a happy piece of information.

"So it had to be from the hotel! She was followed from the hotel. Someone deliberately punctured her tire!"

"That would be a reasonable assumption!" I said.

"Normally I am with her on Saturdays at the beach. It's where I first met her a few years ago. It's a ritual. I used to have a condominium next to the church a pooch punt away!" I thought it was interesting that he was not so embittered that he was able to use that particular metaphor.

"Do you know anything about the Lauderdale Beach-side Hotel patio bar?" he asked.

"I worked an off duty detail there years ago when it was a Howard Johnson's. It probably hasn't changed much since then. On weekends it was a gathering place of the young and the beautiful. Sort of a Sport's Illustrated swim suit issue come to life."

"That's a good way to put it! It's a place where the girls undress for swimming and never go near the water. And for the hotel it is strictly a win-win situation with all of the creep males paying for drinks and pawing the ground!" There was an unmistakable edge in his voice, as though, looking back at it, the game no longer seemed as harmless as it once did.

I got out my notebook and slapped it on the bar. "So your reason for not accompanying Caroline was that you had a network board meeting yesterday."

"That's right!"

"And that lasted until 2:00 in the afternoon."

"Right!"

"And you were alone!"

"It's Margaret's day off. She visits her sister in Delray and usually gets home around midnight!"

"And Caroline from all reports left the hotel at three-thirty and was expected home at least by five."

"We always go out to dinner on Saturday. When it got to be six I started calling around. I called the Coyles whom we normally sit with on the beach and they both said she left alone."

"Then you called the Hillsboro Police at around seven."

"It took about an hour for the officer and me to check the emergency rooms. And she took the initial information but told me that with adults there was a forty-eight hour wait before they would seriously investigate. That's when I called Al,......., the Sheriff that is, and he ordered the tracing of Caroline's phone. Coincidentally cell phone towers happen to be my business."

"And they located the car at Northeast 4th Street just past the fire station and right next to the municipal beach parking lot in Pompano Beach! Her purse was gone but the phone was in the driver door pocket!"

"The sheriff met me there along with your detective Blocker. There is a line of meters along the street but she obviously had to park behind the last car in a non-designated parking spot. It strikes me as more than a little remiss that no cop on patrol took notice of a purple Corvette sitting on a flat after all the beach traffic had cleared out!"

"Or fireman," I said.

"Have you ever run into that ploy before? The puncturing of tires?"

"Back in the eighties it was a common M.O. of the Columbians who would fly into the country in teams to rob jewelry salesmen at the various jewelry centers around the country. New York, Miami, Chicago, Los Angeles! But, as a gambit it went by the boards with the advent of cell phones. Before the phones, the salesman would have to pop the trunk to get to the spare and while he was changing the tire the thieves would pull up behind him and offer to help. While he was being distracted one of them lifted the sample cases out of the trunk. Now the salesmen are required by the insurance companies to stay inside the car and call Triple A."

Lee digested that for a few minutes before finishing off his coffee. "You know that's the thing about Caroline. She wouldn't even call me to come help. She was raised on a farm and was driving tractors at twelve. There is no doubt in my mind she would have expected to change her own tire."

"The forensic guys told me," I said, "that the top of the car's trunk was wiped clean of prints, an indication that it had been closed by the culprit. Unless there was a rain you will nearly always find prints or impressions on the top of the trunk."

Lee shook his head, fully understanding the significance of a trunk wiped clean. "So what happens next?"

I flipped a couple of pages in the notebook. "Her mother is widowed and lives alone in Edwardsville, Illinois. Have you contacted her yet?"

"Not yet. I am still hoping I won't have to!"

"There is a note in the detective's report that he took Caroline's tooth brush for DNA and that her dentist's name is Doctor Steven Paul in Lauderdale By the Sea."

"Yes, Steve!"

10

"And in parenthesis it says that he is a former boy friend!"

"If you are wondering about whether he has a motive here you can rid yourself of the thought! Steve is a friend of both of ours! He is a free spirit! A confirmed bachelor! All some girl has to do is hum three bars of 'Here Comes the Bride' and he is on the first plane to Richmond!"

"Does he frequent the patio bar?"

"To my knowledge he has never been there!"

"I called the hotel and had them pull the surveillance tapes. I want to look at them with you and we are talking about an investment of five hours. Do you have that kind of time this afternoon?"

"Absolutely! I should have thought of that myself. I've never paid any attention to the cameras. How many are there?

"Just three, but only two will be helpful to us. The one focused on the outside bar and the other on the entrance and exit point of the parking lot. The third is in the hotel lobby"

"We could bring them back here to watch on the big screen!"

"That might be a good idea!" I said. "But I would rather do it at the station. Surveillance cameras have come to be a major asset in investigations and we are really set up to do the whole thing right."

"So you want me to go with you now?"

"Yes, but in separate cars. I will meet you at the hotel first. And before we go. Did Caroline stop on the way to the hotel for breakfast?"

"We had breakfast here before she left!"

"And what time did she leave?"

"It would have been sometime around 9:30 am."

"Could she have stopped along the way?"

"Not very likely!"

"Does she smoke?"

"Your thinking that she may have stopped somewhere en-route and that someone saw her and followed her to the hotel. While, the more I think about it, the more I'm inclined to believe that it was one of the regular creeps who saw that she was without me for a change. And no, she doesn't smoke. She should have driven straight to the hotel without getting out of her car!"

"It wasn't a spur of the moment thing, you know," I said quietly. "It would have been someone who left home in the morning with the idea of finding a victim. Not some creep, as you call them, who suddenly took advantage of the fact that you weren't with her!"

"Now why do you say that?"

"The wound to the tire was clean, narrow and deep. Our suspect went to the beach with an awl or an ice pick. Now how many people do that?"

CHAPTER TWO

We took the elevator to the garage where Lee slid into his copper colored Porsche and the mammoth door proceeded to grind open. He spun his tires backing out and managed to constrain himself, with a revving engine, until I cleared the descending door. And then he was gone, down the driveway, up the incline out on to the highway and gone, leaving us with the sound of a lawn mower spitting rivets. It affirmed a long held suspicion of mine that maturity was not a prerequisite to the making of money.

Twenty minutes later I rolled into the entrance to the hotel parking lot where a flash of the badge wasn't enough. The kid needed my name and proceeded to write it in the log affixed to his clipboard. As soon as I parked I headed back to the valet who was standing under a table umbrella.

"So what happens here?" I asked pointing to the clipboard.

"Oh, you mean the log?" He was a young kid, about college age, in a yellow striped golf shirt and tennis shorts. "We have to keep track of the visitors, Sergeant. We collect parking fees on the non-guests and my boss needs to have proof of who and how many! The hotel lets the boss keep the revenue as a reward for paying our salaries and maintaining enough parking space for the hotel guests!"

"So what kind of information do you record?"

"On all non-guests we put down the make of the car, the color and tag. Except for the VIPs and then we need a name, too."

"Do you still have yesterday's sheets with you?"

"Mr. Park has them inside. He asked Joel to bring them by this morning!"

Park was the assistant manager I had talked to earlier and his office was just down the hall from the front desk. I knocked and opened the door to find Lee and him seated in front of a television monitor. On the screen was a picture of the valet stand and the entrance and exit. I decided not to make an issue about their premature handling of what could be critical evidence or the fact that I would have preferred to do the review at the station with more selective eyes!

"We think we have the car!" Lee said, with more deliberation than excitement.

"When she left in the afternoon there was a Hummer right behind her," Park added. The assistant manager was a good-looking guy, surprisingly young to be an assistant manager at a major hotel, and with jet-black hair that contrasted with a peaches and cream complexion. He couldn't have been twenty-five.

Park backed up the film until the time in the upper right corner said 3:47 PM and we had a clear view of Caroline's Corvette exiting the parking lot and turning right. Immediately behind it was a dark colored Toyota or Honda that exited turning left. There was a small delay before the Hummer came into view and the clock in the upper right corner said 3:52. Upon leaving it turned in the same direction as Caroline's Corvette.

"We have the tag," Park said, handing me a slip of paper. "And it checks with the valet log!" Which I could see he was holding along with the monitor.

"Can I see the valet log?" I asked.

The log did not list times but I could see that the car that entered the lot after Caroline in the morning was a silver Dodge truck. Scanning the log I could see that the Hummer in question had arrived five cars earlier than our Corvette.

""Why don't we back it up to, say, three I want to see who left before Caroline!"

I could see they were both a little puzzled by that but didn't say anything. Park backed up the monitor and we sat watching the alternate departure of cars from 3:00 pm on.

The first two cars that left turned southbound.

"Of course, we have to keep in mind that the suspect could have parked away from the hotel altogether," I said.

"Not likely," Park said. We have a bunch of small motels all along the street and the owners are psychopathic about beachgoers using their parking. And as for the shopping center, Sea Ranch Lakes has a cop on duty who is there to tow beachgoers who try to use the commercial parking. And he is a retired New York cop who has been doing it for years and knows all the regulars!"

"I remember that," I said. "And of course the way to beat the system would be to not look like a beachgoer. The cop is really looking for people carrying towels and chairs. You would have to park and enter one of the stores before exiting later and walk casually toward the beach!"

At 3:10 a light colored Honda Element exited and turned north and I made a note of the tag.

"The cop's name is Verdi," Park said, "and he is pretty good at associating people with cars. And he is aggressive as hell!"

At 3:27 a dark colored Chevrolet came out and turned

north. Another notation!

"Well, if the suspect did use the shopping center, it would have to be the near end where the cop is." Lee said. "It's a long walk to the far end and by the time he reached his car Caroline's, theoretically, could be in the outskirts of Lake Worth!"

At 3:30 PM another dark colored Ford turned north. And I made another note of it.

"So you're thinking that the guy could have left ahead of her!" Lee said.

"Well, if he knew her car he wouldn't have to wait until she got inside it to puncture the tire and then have to hustle on to his own. And by being ahead of her he could have a little more leeway on timing in case someone was passing in the parking lot when he was getting ready to punch the tire. He would have headed out to do his thing as soon as he saw Caroline stand up and put on her shorts! The earlier he stabs the tire the better chance that it goes flat before she gets all the way home. And he just might know how far she has to go!"

Another car exited but turned south. So far we had three of them turning north.

"And if Caroline stopped to talk to friends at the bar as she usually does, he could be as much as fifteen minutes ahead of her," Lee said. "And all he had to do then was go on up the road to the restaurant or one of the condos and wait for her to come on by."

"Exactly!" I said.

At 3:37 a light colored Mercedes SUV crawled to a stop at the exit and stood waiting for the traffic to open up. It had what appeared to be an out of state tag with a cactus plant on the left end of it, most likely Arizona. When the opportunity

16

was present, it rolled out onto Ocean Boulevard and turned north! I ran down the log and saw the Arizona tag and made a note of it.

At 3:32 two more cars left the lot but headed south.

Then at 3:47 pm Caroline's Corvette came into view.

I had Park run the tape back to where Caroline had arrived in the morning. He had checked it earlier and knew that the time was 10:05 am. We were looking at a shot of the Corvette as it turned into the parking lot and while the attention of my companions was fixed on Caroline's car I had my eye on the passing traffic on Ocean Boulevard. In quick succession two cars swept south past the entrance neither of them matching the four that had turned north. The third, though, a lighter colored SUV, did. But, instead of turning into the parking lot it continued on south. The log revealed that the Mercedes SUV with the Arizona tag arrived at the entrance at least fifteen cars after the Corvette.

Could the guy be that clever? Could he be so camera sensitive that he purposely stalled around to delay his arrival in order not to be associated with the Corvette. If so, he was no newcomer to crime. I was sure that Park and Lee hadn't the slightest clue to what it was I was looking for and I really wanted to leave it that way. I had Park speed up the tape while we watched a series of cars entering and leaving at the accelerated pace. When we finally saw the lighter colored Mercedes turning in I had him stop. The time in the corner of the screen was 11:00 am. It was an hour after Caroline's arrival. And the car had come from the south.

Standing up I said with finality, "Okay, it looks more and more like the Hummer but we will check them all out! Tom, I am going to need to take the tapes with me and I will need a copy of the log. And I will need a record of any single males that have registered at the hotel since Friday!"

CHAPTER THREE

The Lauderdale Beachside Hotel has two buildings. The main building is on Ocean Drive and the beachside building is immediately to its rear on El Mar Drive. The parking lot is adjacent to the main building on its south side and the patio and pool area are next to the annex, also on the south side.

There had been some obvious refinements to the patio-pool area, since I had last seen it, but the Sunday clientele looked very much the same. There was the usual bevy of beauties clad (or unclad according to your point of view) in the latest version of what to wear, minimally, when proximate to water. In a hotel that predominantly catered to families the weekend influx was a bothersome dilemma. For the impressionable young it was Anatomy 101. But the ring of the registers had, long since, rendered the issue of propriety moot.

Lee and I made our way along the bar while he was having trouble separating himself from the well-meant condolences of several of the regulars. It took the better part of an hour before we arrived behind the protective glass at the southern end. That is where the hamburgers were grilled to order, with huge fans sending the seductive aroma out to the sunbathers on the sand!

"The best hamburger in Fort Lauderdale," Lee had promised, and he was right about that.

We settled in a booth where he was able point out where the Coyle's were lying under umbrellas on folded chairs, not far from the steps. "We always sit with them," He said. "There is a Saturday crowd, a Sunday crowd and a

Saturday-Sunday crowd like the Coyles or Tony and Roger at the bar."

Unfortunately, no one seemed able to recall a possible suspect. What I did learn was that Lee's friends referred to him as "Stod"!

There were four rows of folded chairs on the beach below, nearly all of them rented, and beyond them a volleyball net where a noisy, enthusiastic game was in progress. The genders of the teams were mixed but it was obvious that two of the females, both tall and lithesome, one black, one white, were the class of the field.

"On the ride down here I talked with the public information officer and we are setting up a news release to air on all three local stations as soon as the Dolphin game concludes," I said. "That would be around 4:00 PM!"

"Okay!" Lee's burger was disappearing at a record rate and it was obvious that the stress of events had no undermining impact on his appetite.

"It is vital that we get the information out as soon as possible. What is important, and I need you to remember it is that we are not going to mention the tapes, or any information about a possible car. If the Hummer is the right car we don't want the guy taking it off the streets or leaving town! We will alert our patrol units about the car but we want the culprit to be confident that we have no leads."

"Okay!"

"I mention this because the PIO wants you to head home and be there for an interview to be shown later on the early news. We want to get the portrait over the bar into the coverage! But you have to tell Margaret that we have no leads at this time! We are hoping that someone, somewhere remembers seeing Caroline or her car.

19

His eyes narrowed only slightly. "What about you and I viewing the bar tape? I really want to stick close to you on this investigation!"

"The publicity is more critical right now! I can view the tape and if there is something that can use your input we will get together probably tomorrow! Besides look around you! What you see right now is what is going to be on the tape! I don't expect anyone to jump out at us as a suspect! It is going to have to work the other way around. Once we have a suspect, the tape will be able to show us if he was here at the bar. And there is a good chance he will have gone for one of these hamburgers at some point, rather than walk to the shopping center."

"I see what you mean!" he admitted reluctantly. "We have to hope that the announcement brings us an important tip!"

"The Hummer is important," I said. "And the four cars that turned north before her! I will check them out as soon as I hit the station! But first we have to call Caroline's mother. We can't go on television and tell the world about Caroline's disappearance before she has been informed."

His plate was clean and he suddenly slid out of the booth and stood up. "I need another beer. Do you want a beer? After all it is supposed to be your day off!"

"I'm fine," I said. "Go get your beer and we will make the call!"

It was a scant two steps to the crowded bar where he managed to insert his bulk between two of the occupied stools. The volley ball game had concluded and the tall black girl in the nearly non-detectable swimsuit made her way up to Lee. There was more sand than material across her shapely behind. While she commiserated with Stoddard she

20

glanced toward me several times, before breaking away to saunter over.

"Aren't you Detective Kilbane?' she asked, sweetly. "I'm Veronica Dean! I work in the Secretary of State's office in case filing." The fact that I didn't remember her gave me pause to reflect!

"I see you in there a lot filing cases. You've got a good reputation, too. I am glad to see someone like you assigned to finding Caroline! It makes me feel a lot better about this terrible thing!"

She had to move to the side to allow Lee to slide back into the booth, beer in hand.

"You really stood out on that volley ball court, Veronica," I said. "You were head and shoulders above the rest! Both literally and figuratively!"

She threw her head back and laughed.

"Veronica went to the Olympics a few years ago," Stoddard said. "And starred at the University of Florida!"

"That explains it!" I said, bringing my cell phone to the fore.

Taking it as a signal, although it was unintended, Veronica flashed a pearly smile. "Well, I know you two are busy and I wish you guys the best of luck! Caroline is such a sweetheart! I'll see you back on the farm, Sergeant!"

We took the time to watch her sidle off, brushing some of the sand from her abbreviated bottoms.

Checking my notebook I dialed Caroline's mother in Illinois. She answered on the third ring. "Mrs. Albright?" I asked. "I have Stoddard Lee with me and he wants to give you some information about Caroline!" There was no easy way to do this and her anxious gasp was clearly discernible as I handed the phone to Lee and made a note of the time for the record.

It was really tough on Lee! Dread was written on his face as he made his stumbling explanation. "There really is no reason for you to come down here right now," I heard him say. "No really, Joan. Not right now! It's too early in the game.........the, uh, events!"

When he finally hung up he looked at me with a shrug of his large shoulders. "There was no talking her out of it! She is going to catch the first plane out of Saint Louis. She would have been coming down to see us at Christmas anyway. So she's just going to be a little early."

He drained about half of his beer in one fell swoop. And neither of us said anything for a few seconds. I looked at my watch and it was 1:30 pm.

"You want to know something?" he finally said. "I have never been one to be sold on beauty alone. I always felt that looks alone had the capacity to capture your interest for about fifteen minutes tops! I was always drawn to girls that had physical flaws somewhere. Or brains at the very least! It was the knobby knees or the off kilter nose that drove me wild. That is until I ran into Caroline.

He took another purposeful swig of his beer. "You would have to say that she is as physically flawless as a girl could possibly be! Her eyes are so green that you think you are looking at emeralds! If she were standing here right now in her swimsuit you wouldn't be able to take your eyes off of her. But in spite of it all her ego is completely in check.

"She is mostly about other people. It's her nature to be faithful! I have no doubt about that! Yet she can flirt with the best of them. If she senses that some poor slob is largely neglected she seems to feel an obligation to make him think he is a virtual Casanova! At the same time she has a tough, tomboy streak about her, too, the result of growing up with a father who wanted a son. The only thing that gives me any hope of finding Caroline alive is that the toughness might help her survive!"

CHAPTER FOUR

At the moment I emerged from my car the phone began to play the "Victory March"! And I was treated to the battery acid baritone of Murray Abrams. Terse and ever to the point the Captain had a way of making one feel he was in some kind of trouble.

"Where the hell are you?" he wanted to know.

"I am just about to enter the station," I answered.

"Well, stop by my office first!" he ordered.

I took the elevator to the third floor and shoved the plastic into the door marked "Criminal Investigations". The door to the Captain's office was open and Murray was standing with his back to me, looking out the window, with, as usual, a phone stuck in his ear. Without turning around he waved me to a chair.

On one wall was a framed number 13, with the kind of gold numbers you use to mark your house or mailbox. We all knew the significance. The numbers represented the number of haircuts remaining until he retired, a prospect he claimed to be looking forward to, but most of us wanted to regard as unlikely ever to occur. At least we took turns suggesting that he should start wearing his hair longer than the close-cropped salt and pepper style that had become his trademark. In the course of his nearly thirty years in law enforcement the job monopolized his every waking minute and he had four ex-wives to prove it.

"He is the right man for this job," I heard him say on

the phone while turning around to focus on me as if to confirm his estimate. His eyes had an oriental squint to them that morning not uncommon for a guy who averaged so little sleep. While, between the jogging and the tennis, he kept himself in excellent shape, he could often look, until mid-afternoon, like he just got out of bed.

"Right, Sheriff!" he said with a degree of finality, "We are right on top of it!"

He hung up the phone to lean across the desk. "So what have we got?"

I looked at my watch and it was 3:30. The plan was to meet with the television reporters in approximately thirty minutes, or as soon as the Dolphins game concluded, whichever came last. "Well we have some cars I want to run but I'd rather not make mention of surveillance tapes at this point in order not to drive the suspect underground or out of town. I'd prefer to limit our presentation to pictures of the girl right now. And her car! She is pretty enough to grab anyone's attention and to remember seeing her, if anybody did!"

"That sounds good," Abrams said. "We can always put the car out later if we come up with one!"

"That's what I will be doing next!"

"What kind of feeling did you get about Stoddard Lee," he asked and I thought I detected some slight reservation in the way he mentioned his name.

"I have the definite impression that he is not a suspect in the case if that's what you are asking?"

"I've met him, you know!" he said. "Both him and her!"

25

"You mentioned that this morning!" I said.

"He is a prominent member of the Sheriff's Advisory Council and I've seen and talked with him at several council functions. He goes all the way back to Navarro! He always had a different little broadie in tow until this one. This one has been with him for a while!"

"Why do I get the impression you don't particularly like him!"

"I guess because I don't! He always struck me as a supercilious bore. No sense of humor at all. I kind of got the impression that he had come to believe somewhere along the line that his business success was more genius than luck."

"I have to tell you honestly, Captain, I did not get that impression at all, although he did not come across as a laugh a minute, either. Allowing for the circumstances!"

"Well he is, after all, a fiftyish guy with a child for a toy and, I don't care how much money you have, it would be difficult for him to be that confident about their relationship!"

"It would be natural for him to worry a little," I agreed. "But even if there was some reason to be suspicious he could hardly have had the time to knock her off within the framework of last night!

"Well I can give you at least one scenario within the framework of last night!" the Captain said.

"Go ahead! I'm listening!"

"Well, let's say his pretty little girlfriend, and, by the way she is, or more probably was, one of the most beautiful girls I ever saw. But let's say, for example, being associated with a much older man, she finally got a little restless. And

26

he got suspicious. So she is a little late getting home last night! They get into an argument and he snaps her neck in a jealous rage. God knows he's big enough to wax her with a thumb and a forefinger! So now he secrets the body in one of the many nooks or crannies in, what I am sure, is a very large house.

"Then he drives her Corvette down to Pompano. Flattens the tire! Walks over to the Parliament House and calls a cab. Takes the cab to one of the condos in Hillsboro and walks home from there. When Hanstein or Blocker responds to the house they have enlightening interviews but never check the house for a body. Later he makes a midnight run to the Everglades. Or maybe he hasn't got rid of the body yet. Maybe it was still there while you were visiting this morning!"

He was smiling and so was I. "Lee didn't kill the girl, Captain!"

"And the basis for such confidence is?"

"When he talks about her it is always in the present tense. Without fail! Her eyes are as green as emeralds, not were! She is flawless, not was! She has this toughness not had! This, in spite of the fact that he is more than half convinced she is gone forever. That would be hard to do if you knew for sure that her body was lying in a closet or in the trunk of the other car in the garage!"

I could see Abrams was thoughtfully impressed with that particular example of sensitive listening. And his feet came off the desk. "That's pretty good, James. In fact very good! But I still say I am right! And I say so because I have seen the two of them together and it just didn't look to me like a permanent fit! And for my money Stoddard Lee is as cold as his squeeze was hot! He glanced at his watch and then back at me. "Well anyway we both have work to do!"

And we did.

We have six desks in the homicide pool and a glassed in office meant for me that I had bequeathed to the department secretary. I was glad to see the place was empty because I needed at least an hour of non-interruption. Apparently Paul Blocker, my key assistant, had gone down to the media room to join Abrams and the PIO for the press release.

I took off my suit coat and put it on the back of my chair and went immediately to the computer. The Arizona tag was the one that interested me most! It came back registered to an Anthony Pisano with an address in Fredonia, Arizona and was not reported as stolen. Unlike Florida the Arizona registration did not list the owner's driver's license or give his or her date of birth, providing a temporary delay on a criminal background check. The Atlas told me that the town of Fredonia was tucked away near the border of Arizona and Utah along the north rim of the Grand Canyon.

"Marshall's Office," a sweet voice answered after information had given me what was supposed to be the number of the Fredonia Police Department.

"Marshall's Office?" I asked. "Is this a federal agency?"

"No this is the Fredonia Police Department but we call them Marshalls here! Can I help you in some way?"

I went on to identify myself and ask for a detective to call me about a possible suspect. The operator then went on to explain that the Marshalls provide the line operations but that more serious investigations were handled by the Coconino County Sheriff's Office. And if that wasn't complex enough that she, in fact, was with the Kanab, Utah Police Department that did the dispatching for Fredonia.

"I will have our deputy return your call," she said. "Are you calling from your department?"

When I told her I was she suggested that the return call be made through my department so that the deputy could confirm that he was, in fact, talking with another cop. In less than five minutes I was talking to a Deputy Bridges and listening to a chorus of bells and whistles in the background. The deputy, it seems, was calling me from Las Vegas on his day off.

"The name Anthony Pisano does not ring a bell at all," Bridges told me. "And there aren't too many people I haven't brushed up against in my twenty-five years in the area. But I will have one of the Town Marshall's check it out and I will get back to you."

It was almost 4:00 and I went into Marge's office and clicked on the television. The Dolphins were trying to hang on to a two point lead in the waning seconds as a third down pass sailed over the head of a Jet receiver stopping the clock. There was time for one last play. A Hail Mary to be sure! The Jets sent four receivers to one side with the quarterback back in a shotgun. Faced with only a three-man rush. The quarterback took a little time before lofting the ball high and deep into the end zone where the ball got slapped around in a mad scramble before falling helplessly to the ground. The game was over.

There was time for a few words from the flush-faced winning coach before he was interrupted by the breaking news.

Captain Abrams stood at the podium center stage, flanked by three uniforms and Detective Blocker. He made the case with his customary urbanity followed by the compelling headshot of the beautiful Caroline. There was another shot of the purple Corvette sitting on the flat tire

29

followed by the declaration that we had no suspects at this time. The whole thing took less than four very important minutes before we were back in New York and Joe Rose was interviewing Joey Porter about his three sacks.

Turning the television off I returned to my desk about the same time that Paul Blocker got back to his.

"So what's happening?" he wanted to know.

Blocker was tall and black, although so light skinned that at first you couldn't be sure. He had the athletic build of a halfback, but, somewhat incredulously, he had hadn't played football since Pop Warner. I had wondered how a guy built like him could be walking the corridors of some high school without a coach finding him, but learned that he had to work after school because his family needed the money so he had to pass on anything extra-curricular.

As a cop, on a scale of one to ten he was a fifteen. Smart, tough and thorough, he was an ideal partner and, to be honest, much more suited to supervision than I. Where I pretty much relied on my people being self-motivated, Blocker was far more willing to kick ass. I mentioned this to Abrams once and he disagreed with me about it but I knew I was right.

My cell phone was doing the "Victory March" and it was Bridges again.

"Guess what!" he said. "I do know Anthony Pisano only everyone knows him as Louie around here. Several years ago he bought the one restaurant in town, a breakfast joint named 'Louie's' and in order to keep the name intact he took on the previous owner's first name!"

"Is he on vacation right now?"

"No. In fact he cooked my bacon and eggs yesterday

30

morning before I left for Las Vegas. And what's more his Mercedes is here too, only with the wrong plate on it. It's carrying an Arizona plate that was stolen from a car in Las Vegas last June. You know how it is. People can look at the wrong tag on their car for months and never notice it!"

"And because he didn't realize it and report his own tag as stolen," I added, "the borrower has a green light not to worry about detection!"

"Exactly! The old double shuffle!" After a slight pause he added, "Do you know where the other car is right now?"

I went on to explain to him that we have reason to believe that it was connected with a girl's disappearance, although not positive! But the fact that it is carrying a stolen tag added to the potential.

"We had a missing girl near here almost a year ago," Bridges said. "Around March! She was last seen about one hundred miles east of Fredonia. The girl was hitchhiking to Las Vegas where she had a job waiting for her. Your answer is probably going to be in Las Vegas, though, not Fredonia. Every time a girl turns up missing around these parts it always seems to be linked to Las Vegas!"

"You've had other girls missing there, too?"

"Not in Fredonia but from the other side of the Canyon. In and around Kingman! The guy you want to talk to is a Lieutenant John Forrest in our Flagstaff headquarters. He's been working the case of the girl from Denver. Her name is Lilly Myers." And he gave me the lieutenant's number.

Blocker had elected to leave me alone for the moment but from his desk next to mine had kept one ear open. "That sounded like progress!" he said.

"We have a suspect car with a stolen tag."

"At the hotel?"

"Not staying there but visiting!!"

"In proximity to the victim?" he asked.

"It would appear to be!"

"A stolen tag is a red flag for sure! I would say you are on to something!" he said.

"You met Stoddard Lee last night!"

"I had the pleasure!" Paul said.

"Well you can guess that he could be a problem with the investigation. He is going to want to know everything that is going on and he is very apt to jump in there at the wrong time and mess up the timing!"

"I could see him doing that, alright!"

"Well, we can't let him in on any of our progress at this time. That's extremely important! And there is a possibility that one of us might be headed for Arizona and if that happens we have to make sure that we don't take a cell phone with a number he knows."

"I see what you mean! He is in the business and would be able to track our comings and goings."

"And he would be on the first plane to Phoenix anxious to throw his weight around!"

"I can really see him doing that! He certainly is aggressive enough to get in the way! On the other hand, if my estimation is correct, we are going to have our hands full holding him off!"

CHAPTER FIVE

The call to Forrest in Flagstaff was brief enough. He gave me a quick synopsis of the Lucy Myers case. And referred me to a Las Vegas detective who was putting together a reason to believe that several missing girls were actually the victims of a serial killer.

"His name is Ken Allen and he has been advancing the theory that there is a serial killer afoot, likely raised in Kingman, Arizona and now living in Las Vegas. He seems to be finding threads here and there that appear to connect. You should be interested to know that one of his victims left behind a car on a flat tire! "

"Really?" I asked. "How long ago was that?"

"Six years ago! A high school tennis player of some note!"

As for Lucy Myers, his own case, she was a young girl, not quite eighteen, a sturdy, self-confident ex-softball player, who left Denver without parental approval, to join a friend of hers as a maid at the Westward Ho Hotel. This was in February of 2008. Her first ride took her south to Trinidad, Colorado, where she hooked up with a retired surgeon headed for his home in Vegas.

Her habit was to call her girlfriend in Las Vegas to apprise her of the identification and vehicle of her benefactor before she got in the car. The doctor, who was in his seventies, drove her to Cameron Station on the old Navaho Trail where they stayed the night. He paid for her dinner and hotel room and went to bed early with the plan to meet for breakfast at 8:00 am.

When she was late, he went to her room where she peeked around the open door in her brassiere. He could see a man's pants hanging over a chair and hear running water from the shower.

She had caught another ride, she told him, and thanked him for his generosity.

Later in the morning she called her friend to tell her that her ride had skipped out on her and that she was going to have to find another. Two days later her friend notified the police that Lucy had not shown up and was not answering her cell phone.

Forrest went to the motel, checked the registrations and found one particular single male who could have been the one who spent the night with her. The Las Vegas detective, Allen, interviewed both the doctor and the other guy who was a local musician and declared them beyond suspicion. It seems the musician got rabbit's feet when Myers wanted his name and license to call in to her girlfriend. He was getting the feeling that she might have been underage and skipped out while she was packing.

Detective Ken Allen of Las Vegas Metro was more than mildly interested in my subsequent call. He listened to my entire presentation without interruption. I could hear some papers being shuffled and then the calm deep voice came back on. His accent had its origins from somewhere in the south.

"I am going to send you a brief summary of ten victims. Girls who are missing, that is! It seems that no one but me believes that most of, if not all, are connected. But here and there we have some key similarities. For, example your girl's car was found on a flat tire.

"Six years ago, a young girl from Kingman, Arizona went down to Vegas to play in a tennis tournament. She was being heralded as the next Chrissy Evert. She won that tournament, too. Just sixteen years old. But she never got back home. Her teacher chaperone wanted to stay in Las Vegas for a couple of days so Angela left on her own. They found her Camaro by the side of the highway about ten miles past the dam, on a flat tire deliberately punctured by a sharp pointed object. So it would appear to be another one of those links that occasionally crop up!"

"You have linked ten girls to a single suspect!"

"We have two high school girls who called their mother to tell her they were going out with a college kid named Jerry Shepherd! That's one link. One of them was in Flagstaff, the other in Las Vegas!"

"Ten over how many years?" I asked.

"Seven years! It started with a high school dropout from Bullhead City, not very far from here!"

"And no bodies!"

"No bodies! But that's no particular trick out here. You go forty minutes in any direction from any city in Arizona or Nevada and you will be on land that no one has any reason to be around. Wide-open uninhabited desert land! You don't even have to bury them. The wild animals are only too appreciative of your benevolence!"

"And no leads!"

"Your SUV is the first tangible clue of any sort, if it is, in fact, a clue. Other than that we have only a pattern to try to figure out. To make some sense of!" After another pause he continued, "We think it might be someone who travels! Like a salesman or an over-the-road truck driver! Possibly

35

working out of Las Vegas or Henderson. But we also believe that he lived in Kingman back in 2000. The we, by the way, is me and a detective from the Mohave County Sheriff's Office. And we pretty much have the stadium to ourselves! Everyone else seems to think that we are forcing the facts! Trying too hard to make the connections!"

"What is the connection with Kingman?"

"It is the pet theory of the other detective, Roy Peterson, for which he is getting a lot of grief from his superiors. Back in the spring of 2000 there was a brutal, senseless slaying of a beautiful horse. A Palomino! Someone, in the middle of the night, got into the stables and planted a hatchet right between the horse's eyes and killed her. The couple that owned the ranch had seven dogs that they brought into their bedrooms at night. The dogs barked up a storm when the incident was taking place but they were all inside the house. We think that whoever did it knew that they took the dogs in at night. So both Roy and I are convinced that the guy was local. Adding to that theory is the fact that the hatchet left at the scene belonged to the family. It had been resting against a tree stump for around three days!

"Our theory is that any one who would do such a thing was obviously deranged and not very apt to settle for a one time thrill. While no more horses were slaughtered some females began to turn up missing. We both feel that there has to be a connection. Most of the victims have been in, or around Las Vegas; Kingman is less than three hours away. The last name on my list is also a girl from Kingman. An Indian girl named Angela Birdsong. A cocktail waitress at Bally's! And this was just last June!"

"Why would a guy from Kingman or Las Vegas drive to Florida for a vacation when California was so much closer," I wondered aloud, "or even Padre Island, Texas? That is, if he was looking for a place to swim!"

"Who knows? It could have been about business! But we do have a three-year gap in our list of missing girls. From 2003 to 2006, so quite possibly our guy lived in Florida for a while. You might want to check around to see if you have some victims during that time!"

"So where do we go from here?"

"I am going to overnight you a summary of the cases. Once you have looked them over give me a call. See if anything jumps out at you! Then I think you ought to seriously consider coming out here to review what we have. You might get a fresher sense of things. We need to find out about the Fredonia angle. When was the license tag stolen from Las Vegas?"

"In June. I haven't talked with the victim yet, but the address was the Encore!"

"Steve Wynn's new place. How long has it been since you've been here?"

"I honeymooned there in 1990. We stayed at the Land-mark! And I understand they've already blown it up, although it lasted years longer than my marriage!"

"Well you won't recognize the place," Allen said. "And I seriously recommend that you consider coming out here to check out the Fredonia angle. Not that we couldn't do it from here, but it always helps to have another head in the huddle!"

CHAPTER SIX

We were all buckled up during the slow, steady descent when, the lights of Las Vegas began to flicker above the ink. The festive mood among the passengers rose in concert with the glittering skyline off to the south as we sidled on by. There had even been a raffle en-route and I had missed out on $354.00 by three seats.

The luster ebbed as we plowed back into the black above the desert only to loop around for the approach to McCarron International. It occurred to me that I was probably the only one in the plane who was there on business and a pretty serious business at that. Like the more sophisticated traveler I came off the plane with just my computer, wearing a cashmere sweater, dressed for golf. A very few days, a week at the most I had promised Abrams and I had, accordingly, only a small bag to pick up at baggage claim before heading for Hertz.

In thirty minutes I was at the front desk of Bally's, and a mere wedge shot away from the ocean of slot machines and gaming tables that flooded the main floor. The bellman was able to forego the cart and snap up the baggage without any difficulty.

"Short trip?" he had to ask once the elevator doors closed in.

"Business!" I told him. "I'm only here one night!"

"Well I hope you get a chance to have a little fun to-night! And not waste the trip! We have a couple of great shows here at the hotel!"

We got off at the 15th floor and marched nearly the length of a long hall before he keyed the card with a perceptible flourish and stood back. It was quite a room right down to the chocolates on the pillow. My caddie made a point of sweeping open the curtains so that the dazzle along the strip came into view. We were directly across the street from Caesars Palace. And off to the left, the fountains of the Bellagio cascaded under multi-colored lights.

The bellman seemed happy enough with a ten. "I'm Charles!" he said. "If your time is limited and you need any recommendations at all I'll be around in the lobby!"

I put in my call to Allen and turned my attention to the stream of vehicles on the boulevard below. The parade of pedestrians seemed just as incessant. The lights were overwhelming! If it is true that there is a light for every broken heart on Broadway, Las Vegas had enough to cover the planet.

We had picked Bally's for me to stay because the last of Allen's victims had been a cocktail waitress there. And her roommate was scheduled to work that night, although there was not much reason to believe that she could add more to the case than she already had. My main purpose, though, in making this trip was really Fredonia and the hunch that there had to be an answer there. Jason Bridges, the local deputy, did not agree with me however. He felt that whoever stole the license plate was merely passing through. He leaned more to the theory that we were looking for a business traveler, a salesman or a truck driver.

One thing was sure, though, the trip east through Fredonia was infinitely longer than the southern route past the Hoover Dam.

When I got to the lobby I didn't have long to wait before a very tall, well-muscled guy approached the desk!

His six feet five didn't really need the added boost of the Tony Lama boots. He had a thick head of brown hair, a mustache to match and a smile that was surprisingly warm.

"Jim?" he said. "I'm Ken Allen! Did you get a chance to eat anything? Or were you able to promote a second bag of peanuts on the plane!"

"I grabbed a sandwich in St. Louis, but I could use some food at that!" I said.

"Why don't we have one beer at the bar and see if we can get five minutes with Adrienne. Then we can head up to the buffet that is as good as anything in Vegas! And that's saying a lot!" He had a calm, deliberate manner of speaking with what I guessed to be Carolina or Georgia overtones.

We negotiated a path between the well-attended slots before becoming persons five and six at a nearly empty bar. The room itself, however, was nearly mobbed! If the gambling business was supposed to be off in the economic downturn, there was no evidence of it here.

The grim-faced bartender, though, would have no problem convincing anyone that doomsday was imminent. Our beers were delivered with a somber shrug and Ken and I made the obligatory touch of the bottles.

"I'm glad you could make it!" Ken drawled. "Maybe nothing will come of it, but I believe it's worth the effort. After all this case might turn out to be the most important thing you and I ever did in our entire careers. I've been tracking it for six years, now, and that Mercedes you came up with is the first concrete piece of evidence I've seen. No bodies. No suspects. Just missing girls. Ten of them on this side of the Mississippi and one for you!"

There were at least a half dozen scantily clad cocktail waitresses hustling drinks and they tended to regard the two of us with what seemed to be more than a slight interest as they arrived at the bar. The girls wore gold miniature skirts that left entire abdomens and most of their hips to appreciate. When Adrienne came to the bar she nodded in the direction of Ken.

"I will take a break in ten minutes, Hon!" she said. Adrienne was blonde, with highlighted eyes, a sharp nose and everything else exactly where it was supposed to be.

"She roomed with Alena." Ken told me. "And most days they rode to and from work together. They worked the same shift. But on the fatal day Alena told her she was going to meet someone after work and took her own car. She was never seen again after that night. This was only last June! The 9th! A Tuesday!"

"And where did they find her car?" I asked.

"Right outside in the parking lot. No flat tire, though!"

"And Alena was from Kingman, right?

"Right! Although she had been out of there for five years!"

"My plan was to head up to Fredonia in the morning but I'm wondering if I should detour to Kingman first."

"That would definitely be my recommendation. Roy Peterson, the detective who is sort of on the case, knows the city really well and maybe your car will ring a bell! That's an expensive car, isn't it? A GL450?"

"Very!" I said. "Somewhere in the fifty grand range!"

"There's this! And you should know about it. Roy has a supervisor. A Lieutenant Martin! He is a tall, good-looking product of the NYPD and the sheriff's fair-haired boy. You put him in front of a television camera to explain what you are doing about a rash of home invasions and he has the looks and the manner to instill confidence. He's an image guy. That's why the sheriff likes him. He was promoted to criminal investigations about the time he had his third cup of coffee in Kingman. The problem is he really believes he is a super sleuth and I don't know whether he is or not. He has a framed letter on the wall of his office from the commissioner in New York thanking him for his role in capturing the Son of Sam, but I happen to know, in a fit of relief after the arrest, these letters were sent out to guys who sole contribution was to run out for doughnuts and coffee. I do know he looks lazy to me and I get the feeling that he is as cynical as they come. Maybe even corrupt!"

Adrienne had arrived and the solemn faced bartender rewarded her with a small green cocktail of some sort.

"You must be the cop.......uh, excuse me, police officer from Florida!" she said, extending her fingers more than her hand. Her smile was warm enough but there was a little of the hardened professional about her, too. Maybe it was the mascara.

"Alena was very special. Very Sweet!" she continued. "And we all want you to get the creep who killed her!"

"Have you thought of anything about Alena that might help us since the last time we talked?" Ken asked.

"Just the one thing about the creep who was in here that one night!"

"Well, both the detective in Kingman and I looked into that and we both have put it on the back burner for the moment," Ken said. "The fact that it was a year before she turned up missing makes it less likely to be connected!"

Ken turned to me to explain what they were talking

42

about. "About a year ago, give or take a couple of months, Alena told Adrienne that some guy from her old neighborhood was at one of the black jack tables and, for whatever reason, made a point of ignoring her and acting as if he didn't recognize her. When she returned with the drinks he was gone. Alena thought it was strange for him to do that!"

"She didn't mention his name?" I asked.

"No," Adrienne replied. "I am definitely sure she didn't mention his name. But she did say that he was always a little weird anyway!"

"Is that exactly the way she put it?" I asked. "A little weird? A little weird is miles from just weird!"

"No she said he was a little weird as I remember it!"

"Anyway, there are any number of reasons why he might not have wanted to talk to her at that time, most likely having had something to do with whomever he was with!" Ken said.

"And a kid she grew up with," I said. "Are you sure she didn't say someone she went to school with?"

"No! She said a guy from the neighborhood. No school mentioned!"

In an aside to me, Ken said, "We did the school angle anyway. Alena went to Kingman North and the Sacramonte girl went to South. Peterson and I went through their yearbooks with the respective alumni directors looking for likely screwballs without any luck!"

"I wish I could be of more help," Adrienne said. "Alena was such a sweet girl. She was wholesome as hell, too. We roomed together for nearly a year and never had a problem. She had a boyfriend when she went to UNLV but he moved

43

back to Iowa after he graduated. She wasn't one of those 'can you get lost for tonight so I can have the apartment' types like most of the ones I lived with over the years!"

Adrienne sounded like a veteran and, although she didn't particularly look it, was probably crowding forty. After she finished her drink and left we got back to the subject of Alena's neighborhood.

"Alena lived in a suburb of Kingman called Golden Valley. It is a geographically large development, every bit as large in square miles as Kingman. It has paved roads already but the houses are cropping up here and there in small, well-separated clusters. Mostly modest homes but a lot of them pretty plush. The attraction is its rustic setting. Most of the houses sit on graded gravel and have well water and septic tanks. The amount of people you have in one block in Fort Lauderdale would be spread over a square mile in Golden Valley so that a kid from the so-called neighborhood can he nine miles away. If it weren't for schools and churches the kids might never meet. Roy and I checked out all of the kids that grew up anywhere near her with no leads at all! An older brother of her best friend is at Catholic University about to become a priest."

We elected to have one more beer before heading up to the mezzanine to eat. "Anyway, if we want to keep the horse in the picture, we can forget about any school angle." Allen went on. "When the horse incident went down, Alena was fourteen years old! The horse got waxed at two in the morning a little late for anyone that age to be out. And you would need a car to drive out to the Swenson Ranch. It could be a kid from the neighborhood but it would have to be an older kid not someone in her class!

"Meanwhile the super sleuth, Martin, discovered that the owner of the horse, Pudge Swenson, had run up over $50,000.00 in gambling debts at one of the casinos and came up with the theory that it was a mob hit. The idea is ridiculous. For one, Pudge could just about buy the casino of his choice. And two, anyone who really knows the mob knows that's not the way they work. They don't go after family or animals! If they have a problem they deal directly with you. You own the legs that get broken! You can forgive Puzzo for the dramatic flair in the book but it just doesn't happen in real life. It's outside the code.

"Finally," he continued, "The casinos operate pretty much on the up and up where the public is concerned. They keep records and slap liens on property. They do it all legally. So how a New York cop with supposed experience could buy into this idea is really beyond me. As it turned out, Pudge paid up shortly after and Martin was sure that it was because he got the message!"

"What about Robin Woods?" I asked. I noticed on your list that she seemed to be the only one who wasn't exactly beautiful! And she was the only victim with a sullied reputation. She seemed to be outside the pattern if there is such a thing!"

"An absolute tramp!" Allen asserted. "She dropped out of sight two years after the horse was axed. Fifteen years old! She was a high school dropout from Bullhead City whose stated ambition was to become a high-class chicken ranch prostitute like her mother's sister. Robin was a little on the skinny side with crooked teeth but quickly accumulating the cash to correct her physical shortcomings. It became her role in life to introduce most of the high school boys in Mohave County to the intricacies of sex. They were coming from Kingman, Prescott, and Lake Havasu in vans so she could crawl into the back and be more comfortable in her working environment.

"Her mother had died of hepatitis and her poor father was left with the problem of trying to control Robin. So naturally there were arguments. A lot of them and loud! So Martin focused on daddy as the obvious suspect. It seemed logical at the time I have to admit. They executed a search warrant on the poor guy's motor home; tearing the place apart while the poor guy sat there smoking a cigarette with his bony knees crossed fighting back tears. My counterpart in Kingman, Roy Peterson was part of the search and was convinced even then, that it was a waste of time. That someone else killed the girl"

"What were they looking for?"

"A ring that Robin wore. An expensive ring she inherited from her mother. That the old man, knowing the company she kept and the places she went, tried to get her to put away in some safe place. The ring alone was an incentive to knock her off!"

"I saw the artist's conception in the reports you sent me," I said. "The 25 point diamond surrounded by rubies."

"Worth about ten grand!" Allen said. "Peterson spent two days in Las Vegas scouring the pawn shops! It was when the Sacramonte girl vanished a few months later that Roy started to develop a different theory. He remembered the horse. He couldn't get it out of his mind. He was convinced that there was a connection and that they had a screwball living in town.

"And so he wound up at crossed swords with his Lieutenant!" I guessed.

"Exactly. To the point where Roy was pretty much being told to drop his investigation! Martin couldn't have been prouder of his uncovering of Swenson's gambling debt as the motive for the horse and he didn't want to have it taken away!"

"Or, having gone through the Son of Sam business and

seeing the panic citywide, just maybe he didn't want to see it take hold in Kingman!"

Allen finished his beer and put down the bottle. "Maybe! But I honestly don't believe it was a thought in his head. But one thing is sure! He doesn't want to believe that he may have a serial killer in his midst and both Roy and I believe he has been wrong about that from the beginning!"

CHAPTER SEVEN

Kingman, Arizona began as a way station along the fabled Route 66, a stopping point in the midst of a vast expanse of arid desert! Over the years, though, it has become so much more. Sandwiched between a pair of mountain ranges and buoyed by a benevolent climate the city has not only gained a commercial diversity but has become a gateway to some of the most intriguing tourism in the country.

On Thursday morning, driven by a personal sense of urgency, I was up and rolling out of Las Vegas before dawn. I had passed the Hoover Dam before the sun rose head on and a few miles later was proximate to the place where Angela Sacramonte's car had been forced to the side of the road. The traffic was sparse and it was easy to appreciate her vulnerability. It was more than likely that a cell phone would not have worked from that location six years before if she had one at all at that time.

Angela had been only 16 and newly licensed. And her parents, much to their regret, had allowed her to travel to a regional tennis tournament in Las Vegas with a teacher chaperone who opted to stay on for a few days leaving the young girl to drive home by herself.

Angela had received a big play in the Kingman paper the day before she left for the tournament, complete with pictures that could have possibly whetted the appetite of the local killer. And, as it turned out, she breezed through the competition to take the championship. The trophy was still inside the car when they found it!

It took me a little over two hours to reach Kingman and another fifteen minutes to find the Mohave County Sheriff's office on Saw Mill Street. By 8:45 am I was seated in the secretarial pool waiting for Lieutenant Martin to arrive. When he did show up I could have picked him out of a lineup without a bit of difficulty. Even in plain clothes he had New York City Police Department written all over him. Tall and slender with an incongruous but comfortable paunch, his piercing blue eyes capped a Hollywood face marred only by a balding comb-over. He had a cup of coffee in one hand and a bag of doughnuts in the other and the sight of a stranger outside his office caused him to stop dead in his tracks.

"And you are?"

I stood up and produced a business card causing him to hand me the bag of doughnuts in order to take it. Then he stuck the card in his teeth in order grab the doorknob. Still holding my card in his teeth he took back the doughnuts and waved me inside.

"Fort Lauderdale!" he read as we took seats on opposite sides of a very cluttered desk. "I almost retired in Fort Lauderdale! The wife and I used to vacation there all the time. Do you happen to know a Fred Timmons with Sunrise?"

"I know him," I said. "He just got jammed up for running tags for some suspect individuals!"

"Really?" Martin said with a laugh. "There but for the grace of God go I!"

"So how in the world did you end up in Arizona?" I asked.

"My loving wife!" he said. "She has a sister here who loves horses. I know you have horses in Fort Lauderdale,

49

too! But not like here! By the way, do you have any identification I could see?" He had a Brooklyn accent you could cut with a knife.

He looked at my identification before asking what I was doing in Kingman! As I ran through my story he made a project out of eating his doughnuts before bunching up the bag and making a nice one handed toss into a basket in the corner. Then both of his shining shoes found a place on the cluttered desk while he cradled his coffee and stared at me with something, feigned or otherwise, akin to disbelief.

When I finished there was a long pause while he continued to stare at me with those piercing eyes. Behind him on the wall was a picture of a much younger Lawrence Martin standing at attention, in full motorcycle regalia, while a smiling President Reagan passed by. And next to that was a framed copy of his commendation for his role in the apprehension of Son of Sam.

"You have got to be fucking kidding?" He finally said, breaking the uncomfortable silence. I just stared back at him and said nothing.

"You mean to tell me that you came 2,000 miles across the country to follow up on a stolen license plate? Or because the flat tire caper was similar to one we had five or six years ago? Not for nothing but haven't you guys ever heard of a telephone?"

If my smile was a little forced at least I didn't have to use my fingers! "I've heard of the telephone," I said. "But you know what's wrong with the telephone? You never know if you are talking to a real cop on the other end or just another deadbeat with a badge! You may find it hard to believe that there are actually guys wearing badges who don't think the job is for real!"

50

It was a traditional NYPD expression he couldn't ignore and he took a couple of beats to absorb the effect.

"So I guess you have me pegged as a typical burned out cynic," he said.

"The thought may have crossed my mind!" I said.

"Well maybe a little skepticism is a natural result of experience. You look like you've been around the barn a few times, Kibane, and Fort Lauderdale isn't exactly Sleepy Hollow so maybe you should know better."

He took a thoughtful sip of his coffee before continuing. "Zealots make me nervous," he said. "They can do a lot more harm than good and get people banged up in the process! When I see a guy fly half way across the country because he has a victim with a flat tire and it matches a case we had six years ago it worries me more than a little. And what worries me even more is some hypothetical case-making held together by baling wire! Here we are and you are without a single body or a shred of proof that any of these girls is even dead let alone murdered!"

I let him run himself out of breath while the cobalt eyes were still burning a hole in my forehead. "Lieutenant, maybe you just haven't paying that much attention. Here and there a few things do connect. Enough to make some of us want to take a closer look."

"And what do you want from me?"

"I need a detective to check out a few things locally. Just a couple of hunches I need to work out!"

"Well you've certainly come far enough to check out some hunches!" He said, disgustedly. "Be sure and catch a couple of shows in Las Vegas while you're at it!"

"And I'd like to work this case with Peterson, if you don't mind!" I said.

"Have you been talking with Peterson already?"

"I haven't talked with him yet!" I answered. "I thought I'd better go through you first! But, as I understand it he has been closest to the case!"

"Let me tell you something about Roy! He's not the smartest guy around, not by a long shot! A tough guy! And a hard worker! He's a good guy to have with you in a jam. But, as far as an investigation is concerned, I could give you five guys who are a hell of a lot smarter than Roy!"

"To tell you the truth," I said, "I'm not that smart myself! So we ought to get along just fine!"

"And I suppose we are back to the horse incident!" Martin said. "It continues to crop up!"

"I'm not going to lie to you, Lieutenant. To me the horse incident, as you call it, deserves some serious consideration!"

Martin said nothing for a very long minute before he picked up the phone and put in the call to Roy. Then he took his feet off the desk and stood up making an effort, for what it was worth, to give me the full benefit of his imposing height. "I am in need of some coffee, Kilbane. How about you?

CHAPTER EIGHT

When Deputy Roy Peterson came to the doorway of Martin's office you knew you were looking at a cop. He was as broad as he was tall and stood as if he was planted! He looked like his muscles were more the product of manual labor than lifting free weights and my guess was that he did not join the police force right out of school. Though only in his early forties his thick hair was already white and, like so many sheriff investigators these days, he was wearing combat fatigues so that he was ready to respond to other demands. Considering the Lieutenant's sensitivity Peterson could have been cuter, but it was beneath him to bother.

"So you must be Kilbane!" he said, making it all too obvious that Allen had called him the night before.

"Sergeant Kilbane found out that we had a missing girl with a flat tire five years ago so he hopped the first plane out here to check it out!" Martin said, dryly.

Peterson took a few seconds to stare down his boss before answering. "The fact is, Lieutenant, that we both believe that there is a killer running free who has done away with a number of young girls! It just happens to be a point on which you and I disagree!" It was the calm, non-confrontational tone in his voice that kept him from being insubordinate.

The Lieutenant tucked in the corners of his paper cup and arched another shot toward the basket in the corner and again it found its mark with a clean thunk! He looked like a guy who had played a little ball!

"Well, don't let me stand in your way!" he said. "Except for one thing! I am going to insist that you be discreet in your investigation! What we don't need is to create some kind of hysteria in the town, especially when much of what you guys are piecing together is mere speculation! Do you understand what I am talking about? You can get just as much information if you limit your stated purpose to just the missing tennis player whatever her name was! There is no reason to be telling everyone that you are looking for a killer of a dozen girls!"

His highly polished brogans found their way back on the desk as we left.

When we were alone in the elevator Roy turned to me and said, "I hate to speak negatively about my boss, but he was the lead investigator in the Sacramonte case and he can't even remember her name!"

"It's a New York thing," I said. "They almost take pride in pretending they don't give a damn. He remembers her name all right! You can bet on it!!"

It was my idea to start our day at the Swenson ranch because a glint of an idea was beginning to form at the back of my brain.

We left Kingman on the same highway that had brought me to town only a couple of hours earlier but this time we turned off on the road to Bullhead City. We were traveling along the northern rim of Golden Valley until we turned again on a White Hills Road. We proceeded straight north about two miles until the road ended at the white picket fences of the Swenson Ranch. We turned left to run alongside the fence where a half a dozen horses of a variety of breeds, turned their curious heads in unison as they followed our progress.

It was a pictorial setting that included a rambling homestead and a backdrop of rugged treeless mountains in the distance in every direction. We were in a valley all right but the mountains had to be twenty miles away.

Peterson brought us to a stop in front of the main gate and exited the car. Even though the day's temperature hovered in the high fifties it was more comfortable to leave my jacket in the car. Behind us a relatively dense thicket of pine trees stretched for a considerable distance, in contrast to the surrounding desert.

"Things are about the same now as they were nine years ago!" Roy said, as we took a position along the low-slung fence. Two of the horses loped over to where we were standing to get their noses rubbed.

"The Swensons are nice people. Everyone likes them. Pudge, himself, is a picnic. Always telling jokes! He is the kind of guy who, even though he never worked a day in his life that anyone remembers, handles it all with an unusual grace. The family has owned an airplane parts company for three generations. But early on they bought out Pudge and he invested in this spread and raised his three kids. A lot of people think they show horses but they really don't. Instead they rescue the horses that the owners believe aren't suitable for showing.

"The horse that got killed was named Veronica because her mane kept falling over one eye like Veronica Lake in the old movies. She was another horse with technical shortcomings that wouldn't be obvious to you or me. But the original owners were about to be put her down because of them. Even though she was as sweet and beautiful as any horse alive! Pudge traveled all the way to Scottsdale to rescue her!"

"You knew the horse?" I asked.

"My son, Nick, was one of the kids who came out here to ride. I used to bring him here when he was in his early teens!"

I had stopped petting my horse for a moment and was immediately urged to reconsider by an emphatic nose nudge on the side of my face!

"There was a hatchet," Roy went on, "laying against that tree stump over there about halfway to the barn. It had been there for three days after they cut down a dead tree. That was the hatchet that was used on Veronica. It was about two in the morning. The screwball picked it up and went to the stable and went inside. Veronica happened to be in the stall nearest the door. And he just whacked her. One blow! Right between the eyes! The other horses began to kick and stomp as Veronica went down. The dogs in the house were raising hell, so loud the Swenson's never even heard a car leave, although it probably screamed out of there."

"Were there any tire tracks?" I asked.

"None. Funny about that! Pudge grabbed a shotgun and ran toward the barn and found poor Veronica gasping her last. His total focus was obviously on the horse and the barn because that's where the dogs lead him. If he had looked around he might have seen the taillights of the fleeing car! Unfortunately, I was one of the deputies called to the scene to help place the horse on a gurney and haul her away. In the course of my career I have seen a lot of things that would tear your heart, dead little kids under blankets with their sneakers sticking out, but nothing has burned itself into my brain like the sight of that horse. We buried her out there in the pasture!"

My Palomino now had my tie in his teeth and was looking at me with a clearly mischievous expression. "I know what you mean," I said. "A lot of us humans aren't so undeserving of some of the things that happen to us, but an animal is different. A horse like this is absolutely without malice. Even if he is making mush of my tie! Just look at those brown eyes! Look at the way he is looking at me!"

"You like animals!" Roy said.

"My weakness!" I said.

"Well to see what happened to that horse is to never forget it. I knew we had a psycho in town for sure. And it stuck with me for years. When the Wood girl went missing two years later there was no reason to connect it with the horse. Even when the Sacramonte girl vanished there didn't seem to be a connection. It wasn't until Allen came to see me last June about the Birdsong girl that I started to think about the horse and sat down with Martin about it. He wrote it off as a pipedream and, in a way, you couldn't blame him. But then again it was fair to wonder what ever happened to the guy who snuck up in the middle of the night to plant a hatchet in the forehead of that helpless, beautiful horse? He didn't just suddenly get well!

"Allen and I made up a profile! The experts tell us that animal cruelty is a common first stage for the serial killer. So we figured that the guy who killed the horse had to be old enough to drive and old enough to be out of the house after midnight! But young enough to be in the first stage of his misadventures!"

"So you figured him to be about seventeen or eight-een!"

"Exactly! Which would make him about twenty-six today!"

"We are about two miles from Golden Valley, aren't

we?"

"Except you have to add your half mile up to the turn! He said. "And it is ten miles to Kingman from where we stand right now!"

"As we came down the road I noticed a gravel trail through the woods!" I said.

"It's the bridle trail for the horses. You could drive a car down that road, if that's what you're thinking, except that there wouldn't be much point with a paved road a short distance away!"

"I'm thinking more about a bicycle!" I said.

"Would the killer prefer to ride a bicycle out here at two in the morning just to be more covert?" Roy asked. "Would you do that if you had a car available?"

"I'm thinking more of a kid too young to drive!" I said. "Someone who is really in the early stages of becoming a killer of people!"

"It's two in the morning we're talking about! He would have had to sneak out of the house without his parent's knowledge!"

"Exactly!" I said.

"How young?" he asked.

"Alena's age approximately," I said. "Give or take a year."

I took out my notebook to check an address. "Alena Birdsong lived on Rawhide Drive! How far is that?"

"I'm not sure," Roy said. "Probably three miles or so!

But I know one thing! There was no boy her age that lived anywhere near her house on Rawhide Drive! We checked that out!"

Peterson was turning the idea around in his head before adding, "Well if it was a kid on a bike he would have had to come out of Golden Valley, alright. Everything else would be too far! But could a smaller kid pull that off? Actually hatchet a horse?"

"What's the population of Golden Valley, do you know?" I asked.

"There's almost 5,000 people there, I would think. Spread out over a lot of miles!"

"Back then?"

"Probably around 3,000, I would say. Maybe 4,000!"

"In an ordinary demographic that translates into about 1,000 kids under the age of 18." Not wanting to screw up my notebook I found a piece of scrap paper and did some figuring. "That would be roughly 150 kids between the ages of 14 and 16, half of them boys!"

"That's only 75 boys," he said. That's not an insurmountable sample to weed through!"

"We need to go to the middle school and get the names and dates of birth of the boys. Use that information to get their current driver's licenses. And use that information to send to the Motor Vehicles for their car file!"

"You can do that?" he asked. "They keep a car file on drivers?"

"They do in Florida and I am sure they must do it here!" I said. "If we find that one of these kids owns a

Mercedes utility van today it might mean something!"

"Wow!" Roy said with a shake of the head. "You learn something every day!"

CHAPTER NINE

The Assistant Principal of Golden Valley Middle School, Mrs. Susan Morales, remained unbothered by what had to be an inordinate demand on her precious time. The more so on one of her clerk's. We needed the names and dates of birth of the boys in Alena Birdsong's class as well as the one that preceded it and the one that followed. Black haired, bronzed and buxom, she exuded the well-honed charm and patience of one who has spent a lifetime explaining important things to formative minds. There was a Latin look about her, foreign born possibly, but no identifiable accent.

"We all know about Alena's misfortune," she said after she had assigned the research to one of the secretaries.

"The matter is obviously still under investigation," Roy told her. "And maybe we are on the right track and maybe we're not! But with the kids' names we can go to Phoenix to find out what cars they currently own. It so happens we have a suspect vehicle!"

"So you are absolutely certain that Alena Birdsong was murdered and not just missing!"

"Pretty certain," Roy said. "But you understand that the matter is as confidential as any of the stuff you routinely deal with. We know you can be discreet!"

"Alena left here ten years ago. I've only been working at this school for five. So I guess I can't help you much. But I have to admit that, while nearly all of the kids tend to be well behaved at that age, occasionally we can detect inordinate anger in a few. Boys that are always getting into fights or have a lot of difficulty getting along with others! But I'm afraid I'm not able to give you any help about Alena's time!"

It took the better part of an hour before Mrs. Morales returned with our list.

There were some 63 names. It would, easily, give Peterson a few hours at his desk. He would have to begin by running the names through the system to determine how many of them had Arizona driver's licenses. And then send the amended list to Phoenix. We were probably looking at a few days wait, maybe as little as two.

I could have hung around Kingman to wait for the reply but it made more sense to keep going and wrap things up as quickly as possible. So I took off for Fredonia next. Since there was no direct route across the Grand Canyon, it was a five-hour haul. You had to head out to Boulder, sweep all around Lake Mead and head back toward Utah along the northern route east.

The trip through the desert as the sun was setting was a memorable experience. The rolling hills, as far as the eye could see, took on varied shades of purple and gold. The traffic was so thin in either direction that, at most times, you were entirely alone in a vast expanse of dramatic desolation!

I stopped at a diner in St. George and from there, in order to avoid the winding canyons of Zion National Park, took the southern route to Fredonia. It was a going road that took me past Colorado City, one of the last bastions of polygamy, and on through the oncoming darkness to where the gathering greenery signaled the onset of a city.

From the time I turned north on Main Street I was taken with the little town of Fredonia. It was different from any town I had ever seen before! The main drag was four lanes of highway and along either side was a sprawl of well-spaced comfortable looking homes. There was a fire station, the town hall, a gas station, a solitary diner and that was it. Everything else was residential except for an elegant brick church. It was a bedroom city if there ever was one and in a matter of minutes it was gone!

The road narrowed as darkness descended and I crossed the state line under a blanket of stars. I swept through the outskirts of Kanab and on into the wide winding streets of a snug commercial district abundant in an array of multi-colored trees. At a little after nine I was in the parking lot of the Holiday Inn!

CHAPTER TEN

The scant lighting in the lounge took getting used to but as my eyes adjusted, I could make out, much further along the bar, a solitary female camped behind what appeared to be your basic martini, with an expression that seemed compatible with a death in the family. By contrast, in a booth behind her, three smiley, sunburned golfing types were loudly laughing while making an obvious effort to draw little Miss Lonely Heart into their web. The three faces took turns scoping her out in the faint hope of an encouraging sign. In still another booth a middle-aged couple sat toying with their cocktails in a comfortable silence.

It was pretty much a typical hotel bar gathering on a quiet night in a quiet season of the year.

I looked a little golf-like myself having doffed the tie and donning a sweater before taking the elevator down. There was a lot on my mind and I knew, knowing me, that a couple of drinks would help me sleep, but that three would keep me awake all night.

My attention returned to the girl who continued to ignore the overdone hilarity behind her. She was young, probably mid-twenties, more pretty than exotic. Her mop of red hair looked attractively wind-tossed as though she had taken a lot of care to make it look casual. Her blouse and skirt gave her the appearance of a well-groomed profes-sional, though one with something serious on her mind.

The silver-haired bartender brought me my scotch on the rocks and introduced himself as Jack before returning to where he could talk quietly to the girl! I got the feeling they knew each other, although, she didn't seem the type who regularly frequented bars.

Finally, as if the game had to be pushed along a bit, one of the three laughers stood up and made it to the bar to order another round. "And please give the young lady whatever she is drinking." he announced, his inebriated smile coming off as more of a leer.

His effort won him a slight nod and the faintest smile.

"Why so sad?" her unsought sponsor wanted to know. "A pretty girl like you should always be happy!"

She managed to broaden the smile slightly before answering, "Just tired! A really tough day! And right now I really need to powder my nose!"

You could actually see his mind fumbling for a snappy retort as she abruptly slid off the stool, straightened her skirt and headed for the lady's room giving him and his cohorts something short of a wave. It is funny what a walk can tell you about a person's personality and all the eyes in the room were fixed upon it. Her free-swinging progress was four parts sophistication, six parts athleticism and no parts virginal!

"She seems down in the dumps!" the guy told his buddies as he placed their drinks on the table and sat down. "We ought to try to cheer her up!"

When the girl finally exited the lady's room her drink was waiting for her on the bar. She sashayed on up to it, took it in one hand, held it up like a toast and said. "Thank you gentlemen!" And continued right along the bar toward me.

As she slid on to the stool next to mine she said quietly, "Do you mind if I sit with you for a little while? I really need to be rescued! I am just not in the mood for laughs!"

"My privilege!" I answered making every effort to avoid looking at the three also-rans who had gone suddenly silent. If they really were golfers, I thought, disappointment wasn't really that new to them.

"Would you rather sit in a booth?" I suggested. "It would be a lot easier on the necks!"

"Perfect!" she smiled. "That would be much better!" she said, allowing me to transport her drink for her.

"So," I said, when we were finally seated opposite of each other and introduced ourselves. "You have just separated from your husband! Is it anything you want to talk about?"

Her name was Maureen Ross and she looked genuinely surprised. "Now how did you know that?"

"The tan marks on your ring finger are a dead give-away!"

This time her smile was genuine and very flattering to her. "That was very observant!" she said. "You really ought to be a detective!"

"I've been told that before!" I said with a smile. "I take it as a compliment!"

"And what is it you really do?" she wanted to know.

"I am a detective!" I said. "That's why I take it as a compliment!"

"Are you serious? You really are a cop? From Kanab?"

"No, from Fort Lauderdale, Florida!" I said.

"What are you doing in Kanab?" she asked. "Are you

working on a case?"

"Sort of," I said. "It's really a Las Vegas case, most likely, but we're looking for a few loose ends!"

"Well my husband, that is my soon to be ex-husband is a fireman," she said. "And I am the reservationist here at the hotel!"

"How long have you been married?" I asked.

"Four years!" she said. "No kids thank God! Although it was his idea not mine! Are you married?"

"Divorced!" I said. "A long time ago! You know how it is with cops!"

"Were you unfaithful?" she asked.

"Not once!" I was able to tell her truthfully. "I had enough excitement in my job without looking for more?"

"Did you have kids?"

"No, we didn't, thank God! Her idea, though, not mine!"

She laughed lightly, kind of a miracle considering her mood! "This is a little like looking in a mirror!" she said. "Did she cheat on you?"

"Is that what happened to you?" I asked, neatly fending off the question.

"It's a lot worse than that?"

"Did he try to assault you?" I asked.

"No! No! Nothing like that! It's just that I walked in on

them. That is, I actually caught him and a girl in the act. And I have to tell you it was a real shock to the system. I can't get the picture out of my mind!"

"How did it happen? Or would you rather skip the details!"

She took more than a sip from her martini and thought about it for a minute. "It just happened today which is why I am still in shock! I left some important notes at home. Stuff I had been working on the night before. So when lunch came I made a mad dash home. His car was inside the garage so I didn't know he was home. When I opened the door I could see them immediately. In the living room! On the couch! That is, he was on the couch!" She finished her drink with a vengeance and I took the glass to the bar, wondering how many more she could handle.

While Jack brought me the refills I could see the three golfers giving me the once over with undisguised hostility. The laughter had turned into quiet conversations.

"This will be my last!" Maureen said. "I think it's my fourth but I'm not sure! Normally I would be under the table but I am so angry with my former hero now suddenly turned jerk!" She got rid of half her martini on the first bounce and I thought that re-hashing it wasn't doing her that much good.

"Want to know something funny? The arms and shoulders on the girl were so muscular that at first I thought it was another guy. It was obviously one of his fellow fire persons!"

"What you need to do is take a couple of days to simmer down and collect your thoughts before you decide what you are going to do about it! Sometimes we are able to put these things behind us and turn it into a positive!"

"There is absolutely no way this can be turned into a positive!" she said with considerable emphasis. "As a cop you probably have seen a lot of this kind of thing. Couples in trouble, I mean!"

"Too much!" I said. "And to be honest with you, as much as I would have liked, I never seemed able to say the things that might have made a difference. Mostly, I guess, because at the point when we deal with them neither party is really in the mood to listen!" I took a thoughtful sip of the scotch. I was to trying to time it so that we finished together, "Whenever we get called to a domestic they were too angry to listen to reason or we wouldn't be there in the first place. Our job was to get them separated before they killed one another or one of us! The rational decisions had to come later!"

"My feeling is that if I forgive him he will only do it again in the future? I have no more faith in him at all! It's gone! No more trust! We had what seemed to me to be a perfect marriage, if there really is such a thing! We had no problems that I could point to. We got along! We were financially doing well! It's such a surprise. Such a stunner! And he picks a girl with shoulders like Scwartzenager!"

"Has he tried to reach you?"

"He's been calling on the phone and I didn't answer. Then he even came to the office. I moved my stuff up to a hotel room and worked from there so he couldn't find me. I left him a note telling him that I would call him on Monday! That I really needed a few days to think this through!"

"If you had kids I would say you really didn't have the same choices. There is nothing worse than what happens to kids when parents separate or don't get along. We go to some of these calls where the parents are screaming at each other and you see the terrified little eyes peeking out from a bedroom or the top of the stairs. It tears your heart out!"

Maureen stared at me for a few minutes before saying, "You have a kind face. For a cop you have a very kind face. It's probably what makes you good at your job! You seem to care about people and that's very important!"

The last of the olives went down the hatch and she took another stab at her drink with a trail of a tears welling in the corner of one luminescent blue eye! Then she finished the rest of the martini and announced that it was time to go to bed, sliding out of the booth to stand with a measure of instability. "I think I am going to need your help in getting to bed!"

She proceeded to make it to the lobby under her own steam, but barely, and stumbled a bit getting into the elevator. As we exited at the third floor she produced her room plastic for me and we slowly made our way to her door. After the door swung open she headed straight for the bed and almost fell, but managed to seat herself.

"I haven't got my clothes from the house yet!" she said. "He goes on duty tomorrow so I need to get one more day out of this suit!"

I knelt to remove her shoes as she unbuttoned her blouse and handed it to me. By the time I hung it in the closet she had unzipped her skirt and got it below her knees before falling back on the bed in bra and panty hose. I took the skirt to the closet and found a hanger with clips and figured I was going to lift her legs into bed in the hosiery.

But there she was! Lying flat with her legs dangling to the floor and the panty hose all the way down to her ankles. She was left with a pair of white satin string bikini panties. I took the hose to a chair and draped them over the back.

Maureen was still in the same position, lying there, nearly unconscious with the slightest smile on her face. I lifted her gently and slid her up to where her head rested on the pillows. She still had a slight smile on her face. She was on top of the bedspread but there seemed not to be any way to remedy that. So I got a blanket from one of the drawers and covered her with that.

Her eyes fluttered and she managed to say in a near whisper, "I would appreciate it if you would stay with me tonight! I don't think I want to be alone!"

In another second her eyes rolled up to where they were mainly white and hooded by lids that weren't completely closed. She had begun to snore. I let myself out, closing the door gently, but making sure it was locked.

CHAPTER ELEVEN

My inner clock kicked in eerily and I came fully awake minutes before the wake-up call. I had slept with a surprising soundness considering the unfamiliar surroundings and the added stimulus of the beautiful redhead in the white satin panties. And I was up and in the shower before my focus returned to the more serious matters at hand.

At 8:00 by pre-arrangement I was in the lobby waiting for Deputy Jason Bridges, having checked out with my bag packed and put away in the trunk of my rented car. My computer attaché was at my side.

Minutes after eight the deputy made his entrance, a pleasant looking guy about my height plus a few extra pounds. He had close cropped salt and pepper hair and a strong comfortable face. He was wearing the combat uniform and jacket with the sewn badge and the word Sheriff across his back. I took him to be about my age, maybe a couple of years older.

"Have you had breakfast yet?" he asked as soon as we shook hands.

"No! I was waiting for you!"

"Good! Because I thought I'd introduce you to Louie and to the best breakfast this side of Las Vegas!"

The weather was brisk, probably in the mid-forties, but surprisingly comfortable. Forty degrees in Florida would cut through you like a knife.

Kanab, by daylight was a typically western in every

sense of the word. The buildings were low rise and every street ending seemed to have a mountain view in the distance. And it was compact. It took us only a few minutes to reach the outskirts and the feral land that lay beyond.

We were really moving now leaving Kanab behind in a matter of seconds and bombing along a ribbon of highway that cut through a rugged, near moonscape, terrain about on a par with what I had seen around Kingman. We whizzed by sporadic thickets of white trees and an airport I hadn't seen the night before

"So how many men do you have?" I asked.

"You mean sheriff's deputies? Here! With me?" he asked with a laugh. "Just me, the proverbial lone ranger! There is not a lot of population in the unincorporated area that is my responsibility and only a little over 1,000 in Fredonia itself. For the most part I back up the town's cops in the few instances when they need it and have to make sure during the hunting season that the hunters don't kill each other or get themselves lost!"

"So it's a one riot, one man type of deal!" I said.

"Except that I have been around here for twenty-five years and we are still waiting for our first riot!"

In a few minutes we were entering the outskirts of Fredonia and Bridges began to throttle down to a speed more conducive to the four-lane highway that doubled as Main Street. The crisply clean houses along either side all seemed to have at least half-acre lots to go with them, most of them a lot more than that. Nothing seemed to be constricted. And the idea of a four-lane highway for a main street in a quiet town seemed beyond comparison! It was like saying hello and goodbye in the same sentence.

Allen pointed out the county building as we went by

and then Louie's famous diner where he turned off the road into a parking area to the rear. Louie's silver Mercedes GL450 was there along with a handful of other cars as we backed into one of the few remaining spaces. The van had a paper tag with the former number scrawled on it.

"Louie's only serves breakfast and lunch," Jason told me while we were still sitting in the patrol car. "This means that if you came back here around two in the afternoon his would be the only vehicle in the lot. And, as you can plainly see, it is very private back here. No one can see you! This is where we think that the exchange of license plates took place!"

"You know Louie's tag came due in September," I said. "This means that toward the end of August he applied the new sticker to one tag or the other! Where is the tag you took off?"

"We sent it on to it to Flagstaff for processing," he answered. "But I took a picture of it. If my memory serves me right it had a January sticker along with this year's decal." He thought about that a minute. "So that means the first tag was stolen in June and Louie's was two months later at least!"

"If Louie put his new sticker on in August!"

"That doesn't change anything though! It still, in my mind, adds up to someone passing through, not someone who lives here!"

"What we do know is that the culprit wanted a tag to match his car and that was not reported stolen so that a superficial check wouldn't raise any flags. But the question remains how far would a guy have to go to find a match?"

"Well the Mercedes utility van isn't exactly in a class with the Camry in numbers on the road." Bridges said. "It's a pretty expensive car!"

"But how far does a guy have to go to find a match?"

We exited the car to be pleasantly assaulted by the aromatic blend of coffee and grilled bacon and that, along with the breathtaking cold created an instant appetite! I was starved!

It was one of those diners with a counter that ran its length, with about seven booths along the opposite wall. Louie, a thick set Italian type, did his artful, if pedestrian, cooking in plain view and his morning clean apron was already gathering the evidence. He greeted Bridges with a subtle salute of the spatula as we found ourselves an empty booth at the very end.

In my business suit and Florida tan I caught a lot of attention beyond that normally rendered the uniformed cop who was with me. By contrast, the rest of the patrons were outfitted in what would have to be called western casual and even the women wore jeans.

The place was busy enough to warrant three waitresses, Louie's wife and two daughters and, as I was to learn, there was a son in the back doing the dishes.

"I've been thinking about the SUV!" Bridges said as he prepared to dive into his Canadian bacon and eggs. "I am almost 100% sure that I have never seen a Mercedes SUV around here, other than Louie's. But, unless you had a reason to notice who would? I would be more apt to believe, if in truth we have a killer around here, that the culprit might be from Page. It's only about 80 miles from here. If you were coming from Vegas to Page this is the way you would go! And our one missing girl was last seen a few miles north of it!"

"You might be right about that! Also the guy wouldn't

want the stolen tag to lead right to his front door!"

"Exactly! We need to alert the guys in Page, which happens to be my headquarters by the way."

Bridges's cell phone began to play "Dixie" and after a brief listen he gulped the last of his coffee and stood up.

"I got a call to assist, can you believe it? We have a local drunk who goes berserk about twice a year and it would have to be today! Why don't you have another cup of coffee and relax and I will come back for you when we finish the call."

"Why don't I go with you, instead," I said. "Maybe I can help!"

"To tell you the truth we could use another warm body. You have to see this guy to believe it! He's a virtual gorilla and right now he is demolishing his furniture in a violent rage! His poor wife is out on the lawn somewhere in fear of her life!"

We jogged out to the car and in a few seconds we were turning on Main Street and headed south, blue lights flashing. "This guy's name is Dubbs and he is bigger than some of the houses in town! He is an over-the-road trucker who is gone for months at a time and thinks his wife is screwing around on him while he's gone and she probably is. But the bad news is that he has somehow got the idea in his head that she is screwing around with me! And there is a good chance that she put it there to make him jealous! Which is all I need considering that I am one of the few, any more, who seem to be happily married!"

The house was located on the outskirts of town but, going flat out, we were rolling up to the scene in a matter of minutes! There were two police cars already there and we could see a very heavy set, older cop and a tall, slender

76

uniformed female moving toward the house that had a football field of lawn! The front of the house was already decorated with a kitchen chair that had obviously been a missile moments before. A small gathering of onlookers had assembled to watch what had become a noisy, drunken dismantling of the interior effects.

As I got out of the car, sensing that this was likely to turn into a brawl, I opted to toss my suit jacket on the seat. The two deputies had taken up positions on either side of the open front door a few yards away.

"A fucking whore!" came the growl from inside. 'Leave it to me to marry a fucking whore!" Followed by a crash and bang! "But they are all whores! All of them! All whores! Show me one that isn't a fucking whore?" Another heavy thud!

Standing by the driver's door Bridges decided to try the P.A. system, bringing the microphone out through the window. "Alright Gary, why don't we calm down now. Just calm down! Will you do that for us?"

The sound of Jason's voice triggered an immediate reaction. The shirtless, simian form of the perpetrator appeared in the open doorway, his disheveled hair like a mop in a tornado! I could just about smell the alcohol from where I was making my approach!

"You!" he shouted apparently at Bridges. "You!"

And then he came running with his thick legs churning. He caught the advance team unprepared as he straight-armed the heavy guy knocking him flat! The girl made a late, reaching attempt to strike a knee with her baton as he went by but missed, herself falling to one knee!

For me it was clear moment of de-ja vu. It was like being back in college with nothing but me between a breakaway back and the goal line. And I reacted exactly the same, firing forward and getting a good head of steam. I had the perfect angle, not quite head-on and I heard him yell "Whoa!" just before I hit him. I drove my shoulder into his near leg below the hip and at the same time reached out for both legs, getting one. As I drove my shoulder forward I pulled the leg toward me, and, poundage and all, he went down like he had caught the blast of a shotgun.

Using my arms and legs I wrapped up his legs and rolled him over face down and held him. Like a well-oiled rodeo team everyone moved into action. The big Marshall and Bridges each grabbed a wrist and the girl slapped the cuffs on Gary.

"Don't let go yet, Jim!" Bridges yelled. "We are going to shackle his legs!"

The girl came running with the leg irons and Bridges applied them. I finally stood up and began to dust off my pants as Jason and the other cop pulled off his boots and patted him down! It took both of them to get Dubbs to his feet and half carry him, stumbling, toward one of the patrol cars. The girl opened the rear door of her Crown Vic and I went around to the other side, opened the door and slid across the hard plastic seat. When they got the cumbersome Gary to the door I grabbed him by the belt and pulled. The big guy buckled and slid into the seat so fast that I though we both might go on through and out the other side. I got out and slammed the door and the girl did the same.

It had all happened so smoothly that some of the onlookers actually applauded.

"Debbie," Jason said. "Do not let this ape out of your car until we are with you. And, for God's sake, on the way in, see if you can convince this asshole that I am not the guy who is tapping his old lady!"

"I'll see you people a little later," the heavy cop said with some difficulty catching his breath. "I need to take some pictures here and see if he has gotten any more guns since our last episode! And Debbie, the charge is Disorderly Intox as witnessed by us so we don't need to have the old lady's willingness to prosecute!"

Back in the car we turned ourselves around and followed the girl and her prisoner.

"The big guy is Dan Wilson, by the way!" Bridges told me. "He is the Town Marshall and the girl is one of his deputies! Dan is getting a little out of shape for this kind of thing but a better cop doesn't exist! If your killer is really from around Fredonia he's good bet to find him!"

As we turned back onto Pratt Street and headed back toward town, Bridges appraised me from the corners of his eyes. "That was a pretty flossy tackle," he said. "I would guess you played a little football!"

"A little!" I said.

"In high school?"

"In college, too!" I said.

"Really!" he said. Obviously surprised, considering my lack of size. "Where was that?"

"Holy Cross!" I said.

"The Holy Cross?"

"The Holy Cross!" I said. "Worcester, Massachusetts!"

"Now that's impressive!" And as an afterthought, "How much do you weigh?"

"160 pounds!"

"And how much did you weigh back then?"

"We didn't have steroids, if that's what you're thinking!" I answered. "I weighed pretty much the same, maybe a few pounds less!"

"Impressive!" he repeated. "Very impressive! On the other hand how many guys could you come up against that are bigger than Dubbs?"

We continued right on through Fredonia and on up the road toward Kanab. "We don't have any cells in Fredonia!" Bridges explained. "We have to take the asshole up to Kane County. Tomorrow we will collect him and bring him before the Justice of the Peace where he will be sentenced for disorderly intoxication. He was told the last time that if it happened again he was going to do 30 days in Flagstaff and that's what I expect they are going to do. So I will spend my Saturday ferrying him up the road!"

Both cars pulled up to the compound at the sheriff's office and we waited for the iron-gate to roll open. Once inside the three of us surrounded the passenger door in anticipation of a brawl but much to our surprise Dubbs came out like a veritable lamb. He looked directly at Jason and said in a very apologetic tone, "I'm really sorry I accused you, Deputy! I'm sorry for the whole thing!"

We all tagged along as Dubbs chugged all the way to the heavy steel door without any prodding and where two county deputies took him into the vestibule.

"I have to type up the arrest affidavit so you guys might as well take off!" Debbie said.

For the first time I got a real look at her. She was truly attractive. She had a wild mop of blonde hair, clear blue eyes

80

and stood nearly six feet tall.

"Debbie, this is Sergeant Kilbane from Florida and we need to see you at the station as soon as you are through here!" Bridges said.

She reached out to shake my hand and, looking directly at me, said, "Thanks for your help. I kind of figured you must be a cop!" Then turning to Bridges she said, "I should be out of here in about twenty minutes. I'll see you then!"

CHAPTER TWELVE

The town hall complex in Fredonia consisted of two beige stone buildings with the offices in the north building and the fire department in the south and closer to the street. We rolled into the parking lot right behind the Marshall and he waited until we all went in to his office together.

"Well, Sergeant," he said, with an outstretched hand, "we really appreciate your help. If you give me your business card I will send a letter of appreciation to your sheriff!"

The Marshall looked to be in his early fifties, confirmed by a healthy pelt of silvery hair. He couldn't wait to remove his gun belt and hang it on an extra chair in the corner before sitting down with an almost audible sigh. "It's a wonder I haven't had a heart attack from one of these bouts," he said. "Thank God they don't occur that frequently!"

Bridges and I used up the two seats in front of the desk and I let Jason explain the story up to now. When he had finished I presented him with another picture of the suspect car!

"So he stole Louie's plate," he said, as he studied the picture. "I can see why he would steal Louie's plate because any afternoon around 2:00 his is the only car in his parking lot and it is completely private back there! You could sunbathe in the altogether and no one would see you!"

Then he had an afterthought, "But wouldn't he have to spend a little time around here to know that there would be another Mercedes van for the picking in that quiet place?"

"Well you know how that is, Dan," Jason said. "He could have just happened upon it by sheer luck! In his travels he simply kept one eye open for the right car and the right situation! You're an old burglary detective! Didn't your victims always tell you that they had the feeling that the culprit had been in the house before?"

Wilson laughed at that. "That's because the burglar seemed to know exactly where everything was! People don't seem to realize that nearly everyone organizes their houses exactly the same!"

"Almost the same thing!" Bridges said. "He was carrying the first plate around with him for at least two months before he saw his opportunity. Before he found another Mercedes GL450!"

"Well, think about that for a minute, Jason!" the Marshall went on. "He may have known the license plate was about to expire and waited until the renewal sticker was in place! He could be a guy who spends some time around here if he doesn't actually live here!"

Jason was right about the Marshall. He knew his stuff.

"You realize, of course," Wilson continued, "based on what you've told me, that if the guy drove his Mercedes into our parking lot right now we wouldn't have a case to arrest him!"

"But we would have enough for a search warrant," Jason said. "On the car and his house! That could be all we need to make the case!"

There was a knock at the door and the girl cop had arrived. Both Jason and I stood up to offer her a chair but she declined and took a position against the wall.

"So tell me, Debbie," Jason said. "What did you tell

Dubbs to get him off my case, I'm afraid to ask!"

"I told him that if anyone was having an affair with his wife, which I seriously doubted, it wouldn't be you. Because I knew for a fact that you can't get it up!"

"What?" Jason asked as the Marshall fell into paroxysms of laughter.

"Actually I told him that you were heroically wounded during the Gulf War and out of respect for your service it was something we didn't discuss!"

"Wow! That's just great! I really appreciate that! Especially the part about your first hand knowledge! That really is helpful to a happily married man!"

"Well it worked and he has been sworn to secrecy. I told him that if his wife continues to try to make him jealous about you he could forget about it. But just don't tell her what you know!"

When Wilson finally stopped laughing he produced one of the pictures of the Mercedes. "On a more serious note, Debbie, did you ever see this car around town?" And to us, "Debbie knows just about everyone around these parts!"

She stepped up to the desk and studied the pictures for only a few seconds. "A gold colored Mercedes SUV! Well I may not have seen this particular car but I've seen one like it!"

"Where was that?" Wilson asked.

"Well for one, John Kroll has a car like that!"

"Kroll?" Bridges asked. "That color, too?

"Exactly that color. And Louie Pisano has one like it in

silver! But you should know that, Jason, you worked with him!"

"You mean Kroll. Well I didn't exactly work with him," Jason answered. "I was with him for just a few hours. I picked him up at the hotel in the patrol car and, after I had familiarized him with the town, he dropped me off at my house and took the patrol car away. When I got back from vacation we did it in reverse. I never saw his car." Then to me, "Kroll replaced me last April when I went on vacation!"

"And," she added, "He also has a motorcycle. I used to see him headed out of town on weekends with Joey Rizzo, his buddy!"

"He had a buddy?" Jason asked. "Who the hell is Joey Rizzo?"

"He's a barber in Kanab!" she said. "They got hooked up somehow. Joey is some kind of shooting nut who is always bugging the Kanab cops to use their range!"

I had taken the Golden Valley file in with me for the Marshall to run copies and now I flipped to the list of names. I had run through the names briefly before and could not recall a John Kroll exactly. The first class list was a flop but on the next one there it was. "John G. Kroll!" I read aloud. "Date of birth January 14, 1984!"

"What list is that?" Jason asked.

"It's a list of boys who went to elementary school with Alena Birdsong, our latest victim!"

While three of us exchanged glances Debbie asked, "Will someone tell me what's going on? What's he supposed to have done?"

"How well did you know him while he was working

here?" Wilson asked. "I just about never saw the guy! He kept to himself just about completely. I know he liked to run a little traffic in the morning and then he'd disappear. He didn't exactly put in the time on the streets that you do, Jason, at least not as far as I could see!"

"Did you ever talk with him at any length, Debbie?" I asked.

"Maybe six or seven times at the most. I had breakfast with him at Louie's once. Really, what's this all about? I'm dying of curiosity!"

"What did you make of him?" I persisted.

"Like a dead fish, if you really want my opinion, although I think he thought of himself as a romantic. He had pretty green eyes with little gold flecks in them but, at the same time, they were as cold as ice. There was something about him that bothered me, although I couldn't exactly tell you what it was! It probably was the eyes!"

"Did he ask you out?" Jason asked.

"In a roundabout way! I told him I was engaged. Which was almost true at the time! Lenny and I were in the process of winding down!"

It was Jason who decided to end the suspense. "There is a possibility he may have killed as many as a dozen young girls! We're not sure yet"

Debbie looked like someone had punched her in the stomach. "I will take that chair now!"

I stood up and she sat down! "Wouldn't he have had to pass a psych with you guys?" she asked. You're talking about a nut case here! And honestly I can't see that in him. He may have been missing a few screws but not that many!"

"I guess the first step would be to find out if he was on vacation last week!" Jason said.

"You better be cautious about that!" the Marshall said. "I wouldn't just put in a call to the department and make a careless inquiry because it may get back to him and school would be out! You don't exactly have the evidence right now and your only alternative might be to put him under surveillance! I think you have to pick someone you know up there in Flagstaff who can make certain inquiries without raising any flags!"

Jason took out his cell phone, slid it open and began to dial. "Lieutenant Forrest!" he said to us. "He is already working the case!"

CHAPTER THIRTEEN

At 10:00 a.m. on Saturday morning Bridges and I were sitting in the patrol car at the airport in a cold light drizzle with the heater running. An emergency meeting had been scheduled in Flagstaff for noon and the sheriff had been summoned away from a golf outing in Las Vegas to attend. He would be flying in a Metro helicopter with Ken Allen and an FBI agent, and picking up Martin and Peterson along the way. We were waiting for the Coconino County helicopter which, hopefully would get us to the department early enough to look at Kroll's psychological results before the meeting was convened.

This time I had my suitcase with me with the expectation that I might be spending the night in Flagstaff while Bridges had been promised a return flight. I had already cancelled my Sunday flight home, sensing that I was going to need a few more days.

"You are going to have the rare treat of flying across the Grand Canyon," Jason said. "Even under an overcast sky it is a real experience! Maybe even more so!

The airport, which was halfway to Kanab, had a handful of hangers with at least eight more private planes exposed to the weather. The blue-lit runway looked long enough to land a commercial aircraft and probably could. The helicopter port sat in a space on the inner runway close to the buildings.

At a few minutes past the hour we could first hear, then see the chopper as it settled vertically on the pad. We got out into the cold rain and, jogged toward the plane. Standing outside with the door open was a lean rugged looking guy in department fatigues with his longish white hair already matted in the rain. The name sewn on his chest pocket was "Zink"! His co-pilot, still seated in the cockpit was a much younger Indian looking guy. Alan Zink, as I was to learn later was a career pilot in the service, a reserve colonel, who had flown in the Gulf War.

As soon as we were settled in we were airborne and winging our way above the lights of Fredonia and out across the plains moving through a succession of clouds, both black and white. "Some helicopter, isn't it!" Jason asked.

"I have never been in a helicopter that was quiet enough to carry on an ordinary conversation," I said. "Or one that could hold eight passengers!"

"Or move as fast!" Jason said. "This plane was made in France. Absolute top of the line! We really need it considering the size of our jurisdiction. Coconino County, by the way, is the second largest geographical county in the country!"

"Really!" I said. "What's the largest?"

"San Bernadino County in California! I was curious about that myself and made it a point to find out!"

With that Jason reached into his brief case and produced a thin, manila file. "I had Forrest fax me the application from Kroll's personnel file last night after I dropped you off. I've already read it and, as you will see, the pieces seem to all fall in place. Enough to leave you with little doubt that John Kroll is our suspect. They couldn't send the psych but we will be able to check that out with Major Sawyer before the meeting!"

I had to admit my curiosity was killing me as I opened the file. There was a photo-copy picture in the upper right corner of a round faced younger man with a casual shock of light brown hair and a smile that hovered somewhere between a smirk and a sort of goofy grin.

His birthday matched the one on my school list and the application said he was born in Kingman, Arizona and graduated from Kingman North High School in 2002. He attended Florida Atlantic University in Boca Raton, Florida for two years before transferring to North Texas University in Denton, Texas. He received a Bachelor of Science in sociology and minored in psychology. His work record prior to law enforcement included summer jobs as a Grand Canyon guide and for 18 months after graduation he traveled with a singing quartet called "Hi, Lo, Jack and the Dame"! The group broke up in Reno, Nevada in February of 2007. He went back to working as a guide until joining the Coconino County Sheriff's Office in June of 2007.

His mother was listed as his nearest of kin with a residence in Golden Valley. His father was listed as deceased and in parenthesis it noted that he was killed in a commercial airline crash in 1996.

His references included, of all persons, Deputy Roy Peterson of the Kingman P.D., a professor from Florida Atlantic and a Catholic priest from St. Vincent's in Golden Valley.

Seeing Roy's name seemed natural enough since he knew everyone in town. I wondered how he reacted to the latest revelation.

"We're about to cross the Canyon now," Ken announced suddenly, "although you are going to have to see it in glimpses between the clouds!"

The copter was doing some serious bouncing around as I brought my attention to the window. We were flying at what I would guess to be about ten thousand feet! The awesome formations of rock and sinew below were a muddle of colors, but largely purple. Deep in the bowels, an additional five thousand feet below, the raging Colorado River was reduced to a mere trickle. As the plane doggedly bounced and shuddered through the waterlogged clouds the feeling was one of utter aloneness. Like we were the last four people on earth. It was a temporary respite from the harsh realities that were waiting ahead.

CHAPTER FOURTEEN

Major C. B. "Bud" Sawyer was the undersheriff of the Coconino County Sheriff's Office, but a lot more than just that. Besides being the chief executive officer he functioned as the department's moral compass. He was a straight arrow with a no-nonsense attitude but beneath the uncompromising surface there was an unmistakable appreciation of his men. He was a sixty-five year old veteran with the gray hair to prove it, yet the physique to belie it. He wore his uniform in a manner that was more comfortable than crisp.

The desk in front of him was clean. Not a calendar, nor blotter, nor scrap of paper of any sort. His computer and phone were on an adjunct desk to the side. You got the immediate impression of someone who was totally organized.

When Bridges and I became seated he opened a drawer and produced a file from which he extracted two stapled copies that he slid across the desk, one to each of us. The file immediately went back inside the drawer.

"There is no benefit in talking to the polygrapher or the psychiatrist at this time." Sawyer said. "Because there are far too many who know about Kroll already. We are about to go into a meeting with enough people to fill a diner. But I looked at the polygraph chart and there is one question on it that can be expected to draw a reaction from just about anyone. The question is far too long and worded in such a way that it is almost ominous.

"The question is, 'Do you have any reason to believe that a police department anywhere in the country is looking for you right now?' Just about everyone reacts to that question to some degree. But Kroll sailed through it without any reaction at all. That should have been a red flag. Keeler is really somewhat at fault for not being bothered by a flat reaction to that question!"

"It could indicate that he was on drugs." said Bridges. "Or that he was a charter member of the psycho three percent!"

"Exactly! The irony is that when you are pathological enough to lie your way through a polygraph you should be incapable of passing the psych! The two tests are mutually exclusive!"

"Then how did he do it?" Jason asked.

"My guess is that he found a way to prepare himself helped by the fact that he was a psychology minor in college! And if we looked deep enough we might find that he applied to other departments and flunked a few before he was able to negotiate ours!"

"So if the question is whether or not he hears voices," Jason said, "and even though he does, he knows that the accepted response is to deny it!"

"And at the same time," said Sawyer, "he knows, in is own mind, that hearing voices is okay for him because he is special but wrong for anyone else.

"Which," said Bridges, "begs the question. Do you have to be a paranoid schizophrenic to be a serial killer to begin with? If Kroll's primary motivation is rape and he kills in order not to have to worry about detection he might not be technically nuts! Is that what we are saying?" Bridges asked.

"It's a possibility!" the Major said. "Unless we are to believe that you have to be a psycho to consider rape to begin with. But then we are not experts are we? You have Kroll's psychological summary in front of you. Read it and tell me what you think!"

"On May 12, 2007," it began, "John Gerald Kroll was psychologically tested at this office, his identification proved valid by his right hand thumbprint and a photocopy of his driver's license. The test showed no indications of patholology. It did detect a degree of deep-seated anger that was, however, more than offset by his level of self-control. His intelligence quotient was well above average though not quite up to his own estimation. He demonstrated a rather rigid belief in high moral standards coupled with somewhat unrealistic expectations of the behavior of others. His extroversion-introversion scale was somewhere in the middle, although his sense of humor index was well below average. His authoritative index, on the other hand was well above average.

"In our post-test interview I found John G. Kroll to have the appearance of being physically sufficient to the position he is seeking. He stated that his desire for a career in law enforcement was based largely on his liking for people and a desire to protect the innocent from the guilty.

"In my opinion if Kroll were applying for a position with a major city, his black and white view of the world might prove difficult for him and lead to discouragement and perhaps even cynicism. I would be concerned, too, about his level of common sense in a busier environment. In a quieter venue, however, where experience is assimilated in a more gradual manner his decision-making ought to improve before it ever becomes an issue. This then, coupled with his love of the outdoors, would, in my opinion, make John Kroll a nearly ideal candidate for the Coconino County Sheriff's Office."

When Jason and I finished we dropped the copies on

the desk and the Major stood to gather them up and begin to feed them into the shredder. "So what do you think?" he asked.

"I think," said Jason, "that you need a new psychologist!"

"You know, Jason, I've been a cop for more than thirty years and I would hate to have my job hang on the number of times I've been conned. John Kroll may, or may not be a nutcase but one thing is sure. He is a sociopath of the first order."

"He is a screwball, too," Jason said. "Maybe I am reading into it after the fact but in looking back there was something about him that bothered me. Like one of the cops in town said it was there in the eyes. It was as though someone else had inhabited his body and was looking out at the world through those two little glass windows! It was like he was actually possessed!"

Sawer suddenly stood and, looking at his watch, said, "Gentlemen, it is time for our meeting! We have to go!"

CHAPTER FIFTEEN

When the three of us arrived at the door to the conference room several people were milling about in the hallway, including Peterson and Martin. The Lieutenant half-smiled in my direction and I wasn't sure how he would handle what could have been embarrassment to him. In three days since my visit we had produced a viable suspect. As it turned out he decided to handle it as though my trip had been, if anything, coincidental to the purpose of this meeting.

"How are you doing, Sergeant," he said with an outstretched hand. "Are you enjoying your visit to the wooly west? It's a lot different from sunny Florida, isn't it? Believe me when I tell you it grows on you. The people, the climate, everything about it! I wouldn't want to live anywhere else anymore!"

It was time to go inside and Roy, Martin and I took seats on one side of the table with Sawyer at the end that would be opposite to the sheriff. On the opposite side Bridges had hooked up with Lieutenant Forrest who sat next to a younger, good looking, guy with glasses and blonde hair. Forrest turned out to be around fifty with thick brown hair and a military manner. A ninth guy entered, a shorter, burly type with close cropped graying hair who no one seemed to recognize, but who looked enough like Jason Bridges to be related. And right behind him was Ken Allen, who came around to fill our side of the table.

Each place had yellow legal pad and pencil in place.

Roy, one person removed from me, leaned over to say something but never got a word out before the sheriff entered exactly on time causing us to stand.

"At ease, men," the sheriff said, as he swept by us. "Please be seated!"

Sheriff Vic Rooney, with his physique, white hair and technicolor tan looked every bit the old-time pro footballer. He took over the room as he strode to the head of the table and chose, for the moment, to remain standing.

"Gentlemen, thank you for being here on short notice on a Saturday afternoon. We have taking place today the perfect example of a good news-bad news scenario. The good news is that we appear to have identified a suspect involved in the suspected slayings of several young girls. But the bad news is that he is one of our own. A member of our police department! And to add to the bad news is the fact that, while we have good reason to believe that John Kroll is guilty it would seem that we lack the probable cause to arrest him at this time."

There was a light tap at the door and a matronly female civilian entered and, after making her way along the wall, whispered something in the sheriff's ear. Rooney looked at his watch and told her aloud that he would be absolutely unavailable until at least three that afternoon.

"Sorry, gentlemen!" she apologized as she made her way back out.

"Why don't we begin by going around the table and have everyone tell us who they are!" Rooney said as soon as the door closed.

The burly guy who reminded me of Bridges turned out to be Special Agent Louis Doran of the FBI and explained that he was the sex crimes coordinator for the southwest region of the country with the responsibility of gathering and pooling information for Washington.

The young guy with the blonde hair and glasses was the county prosecutor, Dennis Flaherty. The rest of the people I knew.

"Dennis," the sheriff then said, finally taking a seat. "Why don't you start by telling us where we stand legally on this!"

Flaherty chose to remain seated as he spoke. "Well, as you gentlemen can well imagine, the lack of a single corpse in these cases of missing girls, or, at the very least, an eye witness is a very real impediment to prosecution. It isn't that that it can't be done! But the burden of accumulating enough circumstantial evidence is redoubled and we are not even close. We could possibly convince a judge to sign a search warrant in the hope of finding some links to the killings. Serial killers are prone to packrat tendencies! But we have to consider how unlikely it is that a trained police officer would be stupid enough to hold on to incriminating materials.

"If we were to execute a warrant and strike out then you have tipped off the culprit and he could be expected to alter his behavior accordingly. He would probably resign with feigned indignation and attempt to disappear altogether making it much harder to keep him in your sights. Once his suspicions were activated you would hardly be able to use some of the covert technology we now have to track him and he might well be capable of ceasing operations altogether, or at least until things cooled off.

"Right now you have an option of keeping him under surveillance without his suspicion with the hope that, sooner or later, something useful would present itself up to, and possibly including, an attempted murder! It would be an expensive undertaking for sure and not without considerable risks but it might be our best alternative!"

He looked around the table for emphasis, and finally

said with a shrug, "That's about where we are!"

The sheriff leaned forward and said, "Lou!"

"The burly guy stood up and, instead of remaining by his seat causing half of us in the room to strain our necks, moved easily to a more accessible location where only the Sheriff needed to swivel his chair. And, like any experienced public speaker, he took a few moments to think, looking at the floor before turning around to face us.

"When we are called to a crime scene with a murdered victim the very first thing we consider is motive!" He was a mover! And as he moved all of our heads followed him in unison.

"The first question is always who stood to gain from what happened here? And if that doesn't quite fit with the evidence before us we might wonder whom did this victim provoke! But when we have elements with which we are too familiar and smacks of a serial killer the question of motive goes by the board!

"There is every chance that there will be nothing to connect the murderer to the victim! And the motive is locked away in the recesses of a sick mind!

"In these cases we must rely on the physical evidence at hand or the testimony of witnesses to show us the way!

"Now in the case of John Kroll we do not even have that with which to work. We have no bodies and no crime scene! We are left with only the opportunities!

"Our suspect grew up in a town that claimed three victims, an experience he shared with 50,000 others. But he owns a gold Mercedes, a duplicate of one seen in the parking lot of a hotel from which another victim disappeared! And the vehicle in question had a license plate that was stolen from Fredonia where our suspect worked. And by Monday I would expect that his financial records will prove that he was in Fort Lauderdale on October 17th!

"Now that would seem, at first glance, like a wealth of circumstantial evidence, although I assure you that under a court system that requires proof beyond a reasonable doubt this case could easily be defended!

"Still it is enough, in my opinion, to justify a surveillance that would require an enormous expenditure and could last six months or more!"

"The blunt truth is that in the end we might have still one more corpse to show for it, although, we will be able to say we were there and we can prove he did it!

"Stop and think about it! We cannot drop the net on John Kroll while he and a would-be victim are discussing the latest fashions over tea! We will not be able to pull up a chair and wait for the moment he has his hands wrapped around the victim's throat!

"We are going to have to allow him the freedom to do his thing and hope that our timing is so right that we are able to intervene at precisely the right moment!

"Now if the onset involves a kidnapping, we would make the arrest right then. We would have our case! But if the victim goes along for the ride willingly, how long do we give him to put himself in an incriminating position? Ten minutes? Fifteen?

Doran could have chosen to answer some of those questions, but instead he had arrived at his chair with much the same skill that the wily Willie Pep used to maneuver his opponent into his own corner at the end of a round! He pulled out his chair and sat down allowing the critical questions to hang like an errant curveball. It had a very dramatic impact on the room and it was intended to do so!

"Any thoughts on how to proceed, gentlemen? The Sheriff asked quietly.

It was Forrest who spoke first. "The suggestion of a long term surveillance would seem, at first glance, to be a viable option, but the political consequences of Kroll knocking off some girl while we were doing it would be devastating! I can just see her parents, on television, blaming us for allowing it to happen! Consider the fact that we have no idea of his M.O. Does he take time with the victim to satisfy his perversions before he lowers the fatal boom or does he kill them right off the bat. Take the incidence of Bundy at Florida State University. He just followed the girl to the sorority house, walked in with a bat and bludgeoned her to death! If we had Bundy under surveillance it would have been impossible to placate the parents with the justification that she was sacrificed in order to save future victims!"

"It would take some explaining alright and we would be open to some excruciating criticism," admitted the sheriff, "but what choice do we have?"

"For one thing," Sawyer said, "we wouldn't have any trouble explaining why we weren't able to arrest him beforehand. The evidence is threadbare at this point!"

"Forgive me, Major," persisted Forrest, "but we would have a hard time even selling that! It's been my experience that the public believes that we can arrest anyone we believe is guilty regardless of a lack of evidence!"

"Not that I'm suggesting it," Lieutenant Martin said, "but if we went the search warrant route it might be easier all around! If we struck out on the search you can bet that Kroll's next move would be to resign with great indignation and get the hell out of Dodge! And you could grease the wheels by offering him a generous severance to get him out of your hair! Down the road if he does get arrested he will be tagged as a former deputy and that goes down a lot easier than having him arrested while he is currently on the job!"

"That would certainly be the expedient thing to do," the Sheriff said. "And there is every temptation to do it that way! But I have to say that I am going to have to be willing to take the political punches that are sure to come with taking the proper course of action! We are talking about future victims here! And the surveillance seems to me to be the right thing to do!"

"Why then don't I make it easier for all of you," Doran said, speaking up. "Why don't we make it a Bureau task force and put me in charge. We'll make it a multi-agency squad and the Bureau will take the heat! We are big enough to handle it and not have to worry about political consequences!"

"You would be able to make that kind of investment of your time?" the sheriff asked.

"That's my job!" the agent answered. "And I can't think of anything more important right now, can you?"

"Have you done this sort of thing before?" Rooney asked. "The surveillance type thing I mean!"

"Not really! Not me personally! But the Bureau is doing a lot of this sort of thing right now with suspect terrorists!" he said. "Unfortunately we do not have that kind of personnel available for other assignments because of our current preoccupation with terrorism! But there are probably some in this room who have done this sort of thing!"

I looked around to see if anyone jumped out on that but nobody did.

"I suppose most of us have had a tail job at some time or other," Allen said. "If that's what you mean!"

Again some quiet before I finally spoke up.

"I worked anti-crime for five years," I said. "And that is what we did primarily. Bird-dogging of known suspects and surveillances of vulnerable locations!"

"And who exactly would you be bird-dogging?" the sheriff asked.

"Robbery and burglary suspects mostly. But some times mob figures! The techniques are all the same. The paranoia level of the mob figures made it a little different! Tracking devices were out of the question with them!"

"So how many men would you estimate we would need for this relatively long-term project, Sergeant," he asked.

"Five," I said without hesitation. "You would need two men each shift working twelve hour shifts, seven days per week! You would need a fifth as a swing man to give everyone a week off after four!"

The sheriff brought out a pen and made some notes on the legal pad. "You're talking about 84 hours per week per man. Considering the cost of overtime and the wear and tear on the personnel wouldn't we better off breaking that down with a few more people?

"The fewer the better on a project that demands utmost secrecy. And you need a type of man who is eminently disciplined, who doesn't know the meaning of the word boredom. It's no job for some lover-boy who has his head in the clouds! You are lucky if you have half dozen men in your entire department who would meet those requirements. Like the Lieutenant suggested, if Kroll pulls off a killing right under our noses it better not include a question of

103

negligence!"

"We probably could draw most of our squad from around this table," Doran observed. "And limit the number of people in the know! If we talked with your Sheriff would you be willing to stick around, Sergeant Kilbane?"

"Absolutely," I answered.

"Deputy Bridges?"

"Absolutely,"

"How about you, Deputy?" he asked Peterson.

"I don't think you could use me!" Peterson said, "Unfortunately Kroll knows me. If he were to see my kisser in town it would certainly get him to wondering!"

All heads turned toward Allen who shook his head sadly. "Very regretfully I have three murder cases coming to trial next month, all of them dependent upon my testimony! I might be available after that!"

"Lieutenant Martin has a department to run, so I am sure he is out of the question." The Sheriff said.

"Why don't I volunteer my brother as the fourth?" Flaherty said. He did ten years with this department before joining me as a special investigator! Most of you here know him well! And he is currently single!"

"Richard would be a perfect choice," Sawyer said.

"Let me add one thought!" I said. "Since you would have to replace Jason anyway, why don't we transfer Kroll to Fredonia. He would be alone and unsupervised, which might speed up his opportunities. The area is much less complicated as far as keeping him under surveillance. And it is an hour and a half closer to Las Vegas which seems to be his major preserve!"

"How would we accomplish that without raising flags!" Forrest said, once again the devil's advocate.

After a thoughtful pause around the table, Doran spoke up again. "We will tell him that Bridges has been assigned to a federal task force investigating a sensitive matter for the Mormon Church. And that he is being sent to Fredonia to replace Bridges on a temporary basis."

"He would be the logical choice," Major Sawyer added, "since he was the one who filled in for Jason on his vacation before. There wouldn't be any reason for him to be suspicious about that. And, in fact, knowing him, he will jump at the chance."

"We should have Lieutenant Gray break it to Kroll," the Sheriff said. "And I recommend that we keep the Lieutenant out of the loop on this so that he can't kill us with bad acting."

"Just one question comes to mind, Sergeant Kilbane!" Sawyer said. "You knew about the Mercedes back in Florida. Did you, by any chance, put the description out to the public?"

"On a hunch we held it back!" I said. "We lucked out on that one! The only thing we told the media was that we had a missing girl whose car was found on a flat tire and there were no leads! We didn't want to chase the suspect out of town!"

"Then the last question is, when is Deputy Kroll due back to work?" asked the Sheriff.

"Tomorrow!" Sawyer said. "Tomorrow at 3:00 pm!

"Deputy Bridges, are you planning to be back in Fredonia tonight?" Doran asked.

"That's the plan!" he said.

"Well we need you to spend tomorrow finding a place for four of us to stay. The Bureau will pick up the tab but we need some apartments, if we can get them with a four month minimum commitment!"

"And", I interjected, "thinking of everything, we should get the stolen tag out of evidence and put it back on Louie's car. And when his new tag comes through tell him to hold off on it for a couple of weeks."

"That's good thinking," the Sheriff said. "If Kroll sees the stolen license plate still in place it will convince him that the coast is clear!"

"Which reminds me," Lieutenant Forrest said, "did we put Louie's plate into the computer as stolen?"

"Yes!" Bridges answered.

"Well we need to get it back out! The first thing Kroll is going to do when he gets back in his patrol car is run that tag to see if it is still clear! I would go right down to communications and do that right now!"

"How many cars do we need for this operation?" Sawyer asked.

Heads were turning in my direction. "Four would be ideal. Run of the mill sedans, nothing flashy, neutral colors, reliable but the older the better! And with windows heavily tinted! And," I added, "we will need to plant a GPS transmitter on the Mercedes!"

"I'll get Doyle to assemble the cars and equipment,"

said Sawyer. "Let's plan on having George meet with Kilbane and Flaherty tomorrow."

"You will only have two drivers at this end," Doran said, "so why don't you let me bring the third car up from our motor pool in Las Vegas. When you get your swing man be can bring the fourth car to Fredonia!"

"Your swingman, Major," the Sheriff said," is going to have to be someone that Kroll hasn't met. Do you have anyone in mind?"

"Not yet, but I will have the fifth man on his way down there by Monday!"

"Then that's it!" the Sheriff said, as he stood. "We have a plan! And I will leave it to Major Sawyer to pick up any loose ends.

"Gentlemen," he added, looking meaningfully around the table, "there are eight people in this room and two more in Fredonia who know that John Kroll is a suspect! It has to stay exactly that way. We do not discuss it within our departments, with our wives, our mistresses, our dogs or cats. As of now, John Kroll, oddball that he may be, is a deputy in good standing. And," he concluded. "This meeting never took place!"

CHAPTER SIXTEEN

At 9:00 am sharp a muscular, florid-faced deputy named George Doyle came through the door of the small conference room carrying a large square brief case and plunked it down beside the lead chair. He appeared, with his silvery hair, to be on the near side of sixty but with enough gas left in his system to clean out a barroom by himself. The story was that he had caught a knife under the ribs in a New Year's brawl that had come close to taking him out, but had extended his career by a move into forensics.

Richard Flaherty had just introduced himself before the intrusion and I made note of the fact that he bore little physical resemblance to his brother. Richard was taller and more slender, a redhead with a sly sense of humor! He looked to me like someone who would be easy to live with for the next few months and I was kind of hoping to be teamed with him!

"You have two Chevy's in front of the building," Doyle said tossing a set of keys to each of us. Sitting down he unclipped the brief case and reached inside. "Have either of you used the GPS tracking devices before?"

He got a no from Richard and a yes from me.

"Let's start with the receivers first!" he said, and took out a box that held four of them. Removing one of them he held it up for us to see. "It is exactly like the GPS trackers you might have in your own car except that it is monitoring the location of the transmitter that will be attached to the subject's car. Not your own. It has a cute little car for a cursor! It has a pleasant female voice that will give you instructions just like the other systems. However, the destination she directs you to will always be the target car."

"There are four channels, only three of which will come into play. Channel one will be the fixed on the patrol car being used in Fredonia with its built in transmitter. While channel two will be affixed to the transmitting device on the suspect's car." He looked from one of us to the other. "That much is simple enough, right?"

"I found out he's got a motorcycle, too!" I said.

"Well there is no way we are going to get away with applying a transmitter to the bike. But the upside is that it is pretty unlikely that he can do his act working off a motorcycle. Unless the girl goes willingly into the boondocks with him and he is the kind who settles for a very quick kill without any of the usual formalities!"

"Unfortunately we can't be sure that isn't the way he works!" I persisted.

"Which brings us to channel three and this is just a trifle complicated! Channel three is fixed to his cell phone!" He turned on his receiver and went to channel three, to a blank screen with the message trailing along the lower half that repeated "No signal at this time."

"He is either in a dead area right now or his cell phone is turned off. Do either of you know about radio towers and how they affect the cell phone tracers?"

We both shook our heads.

"They are built according to demand and, in turn, the phone companies subscribe to the towers when the number of clients warrants the investment. In other words you may have a tower in East Overshoe but Kroll's cell phone company may not use it. Everything is ruled by the number of available subscribers, which means that in the southwest there are a lot of dead areas. We have more than three towers in Flagstaff for the purpose of triangulation and we would be able to narrow his current location here to within twenty yards. But a tower standing alone would be able to tell you how close the phone was to that single tower out to thirty-five miles. But in a complete circle." He made a small dot and drew a circle around it to illustrate. "You cannot tell which direction the phone is, only the distance from the tower.

"But if there is another tower within thirty-five miles the point at which the circles intersect can narrow his location to within 100 yards. He might be five miles from one tower and thirty miles from the other!" He drew another dot with a smaller circle that intersected. "It takes three intersecting towers to narrow his location to within twenty yards.

"We have one tower in Page and one in Kanab so if you are traveling from one to the other you would have a dead area of around 20 miles. But if you knew your subject was traveling Alternate 89 you could use the highway itself as your intersecting line!" He went back to the original single tower drawing and drew a line representing the highway. "Wherever the highway intersects with the circle would be where he was! Is everyone clear on that?" he asked.

"I got it!" I said. Flaherty looked a little less certain.

Next came a second box holding two black anodized transmitters each about the size of a package of cigarettes. "Now comes the tricky part!"

Taking one of the transmitters out he went on. "The transmitter is magnetic and you can attach it to any part of the underbody of your suspect vehicle. The closer you get to the middle the better for concealment. In the trunk of one of your cars is one of those dollies that auto mechanics use for attaching the transmitter. Once attached the battery has a life span of two weeks. In the box is a charger for your alternate battery. We are suggesting that you make your changes in the early morning between four and five and that you do not wait until you are near the end of your two weeks. I would start looking for the best opportunity at the beginning of your second week.

"And we have one more suggestion that is going to be difficult to go along with. We are suggesting that you wait a week before you attach the first transmitter. This is just in case he has any suspicions about his new assignment and decides to have his vehicle checked for bugs! Once he feels he is in the clear it should be a breeze. You don't have to have him anywhere in sight most of the time. You merely need to analyze his patterns and react to deviations from the norm."

"Like," Flaherty said, "he leaves the highway and heads out into the hinterland!"

"Exactly! Are there any questions about any of this so far?"

We both shook our heads.

He brought out a third box. "Two department radios and one charger so that you can hear the dispatches that come out of Page! And I am giving each of you an index card that has the cell phone numbers of the other players and you will want to program them for easy access as soon as you can."

There was more! "Two chargers with converters so that you can monitor his activity from your motel room.

Doyle then put everything back in the boxes and put the boxes back into the brief case. "All yours!" he said standing up! "And Major Sawyer wants to see you before you go!"

I took the brief case as we followed Doyle out of the room and down the hall to the major's office.

"I don't have to tell you how much we have riding on this project," Sawyer told us when we took our seats. "So I won't bother to try! But don't let up for a single minute. Make sure that this guy's movements are being tracked at every minute of the day and night. We don't get bored! We don't allow ourselves to ever be distracted. Now go get him and get him cold!"

Downstairs my keys fit the black Caprice and Flaherty's belonged to the tan. And we were off.

Like everything else I found in the southwest there was adventure at every turn. The trip north from Flagstaff was a gradual steady descent from 7,000 feet above sea level to the desert floor. Down to what had been at one time the bottom of Lake Bonneville, a body of water that extended all the way up to the salt flats west of the City of Salt,Lake. The former lake had become pure Indian country, a long stretch of highway through the Painted Desert and on through its barren aftermath eventually to bisect the Navajo Trail.

We had been going about an hour with Flaherty in the lead when my cell phone provided me with a stirring rendition of "Eye of the Tiger"! It was Flaherty!

"We are about to pass a generating plant on the left," he said. "That is where Kroll's motor home is parked. And we could see his SUV parked there if he is back. He is due on duty at 3:00 this afternoon!"

"Okay!"

"There is a crazy idea floating around in the back of my brain that I would like to talk to you about!"

I had an idea what he might be thinking about. "Go ahead!" I said.

"Why don't we stop for lunch at the Indian station up ahead and we can talk it over!"

"Okay!" It was like reading his mind. I had a hunch that Rich was thinking about doing a North End search on the trailer and possibly saving the entire program a lot of time and money. It was also a crazy idea that could possibly blow up in our faces.

I could see the generating plant coming up set well back from the highway. And as we passed we could see the motor home up close enough to the building to tap into its resources. And the gold Mercedes was parked in front! And next to it was the marked patrol unit.

In a few more minutes Cameron Station loomed up on our left.

It was an Indian way station that had a restaurant, a motel and a gas station all operated by Native Americans. Alongside was a penned area that had livestock, where a dumpy florid-faced cowboy with white hair and a Buffalo Bill goatee was leaning over the fence talking to a short bow-legged Indian. As we got out of our cars and stretched our legs we could see the little Indian slide through the opened gate and, with a handful of running steps, corral a young lamb. With the rope securely around the lamb's neck, he half dragged the reluctant animal over to his pick-up truck, where his two young sons helped him lift the little animal on to the back. They flipped up the rear and joined their mother in the truck before taking off out to the highway in a huge trail of dust.

Both Flaherty and I were drawn to the penned area out of curiosity, where the old cowboy stood watching the truck

113

swirl into the distance.

"Them are Hopi," he said, somewhat absently as he watched the truck barrel toward the horizon throwing up occasional puffs of dust. "They live way back in the hills! And they are as different from the Navajo as the Swedes are from Sicilians! Different as night and day! The Navajo are taller, more aristocratic! And the Hopi are shorter and more plain!"

Neither Flaherty nor I felt like prying into that particular prejudice if that's what it was, so we let it ride! After taking a few moments to enjoy the spectacle of the baaing sheep and the venerable old relic of the west who was by now using a large cloth to wipe the sweat out of his eyes, we headed back to the restaurant where we had our choice of seating. It was the off-season and the small numbers of guests were more travelers than tourists. The working staff was entirely Indian. "At this time of year," Flaherty said, "for miles around, the Indians outnumber the whites by a hundred to one. So if you want to keep that blond head of hair in place you better behave yourself! "

We didn't say much until we ordered lunch and Flaherty opened the conversation. "One of the great pastimes around here is to take a dune buggy out into the desert and ride the dunes. The dunes stand about twenty to forty feet high and you drive straight at them. The buggy will slam straight into them, rise up and climb to the top and you sail out into the air on the other side before finally touching down. It's all very thrilling! Of course if you break down out there without a cell phone you have one hell of a walk back in the blazing sun. It happened to me once."

"So what is the idea that's been plying your brain?" I asked.

"Have you ever done a covert exploratory search before? You know, to find out beforehand if there was a basis to get a warrant?"

"Actually, and off the record, I've done a few, especially when I am trying to find someone who has apparently bailed out on us!"

"Well, we are actually in no hurry to get to Fredonia and I thought that maybe we could hang around here until Kroll goes on duty this afternoon and take a look around the trailer. If we were to find he had something incriminating in that trailer of his then the search warrant would be no gamble at all! And it would shorten this whole process!"

"The trailer is probably in the middle of his zone isn't it?"

"Yes," he said.

"Then it's way too risky. He could head up the highway and see our car."

"We would have to hide the car and walk in through the woods!" he said.

I thought about it for a little bit. Turned it around in my mind. But it still kept coming up as not worth the risk. Even if Kroll didn't catch us in the act he might well be paranoid enough to set up some traps in the trailer that would let him know that someone had been there.

"The gas station up the road would rent us a dune buggy and, since we are cops maybe we could get one on the arm. Anyway it would be a fun way to kill a couple of hours while we wait around for him to go on duty!"

"It's tempting!" I admitted. "But the other thing is that we are officially members of an FBI task force and we would be going way out on a limb to try something like this without clearing it! We could be jeopardizing the whole operation!"

Flaherty was obviously the kind of guy who took his disappointments in stride! "Well, it was just a thought!" he said with a shrug.

"Do you think they will move the trailer to Fredonia?" I asked. "It is mobile!"

"As I understand it, no! As far as Kroll knows his transfer to Fredonia is temporary. They are probably going to put him up at the same motel he stayed at before when he filled in for Bridges. I know what you are thinking. That maybe Forrest could do the search because most of his stuff will still be there"

"But he would never leave anything incriminating behind, would he?" I asked.

"He might! He will move what he needs to live with for the next few months and pretty much have to leave the rest of his stuff behind."

"Well, we could run it by Doran," I said. "The thing that would worry me is if he has the place booby trapped! And he probably does!"

"That would be something else to worry about." Flaherty said. "And, if we might speak of the devil, and allow me to do so, and I am sure you know enough not to turn around! John Kroll has just entered the restaurant and he is taking a seat at a table by the window!"

"Are you sure?"

"He looks just like the pictures I've seen!"

I polished off the rest of my sandwich and stood up. "My turn at the men's room" I said. I'll be right back!"

When I came out Flaherty was already at the register with the check and the walk to join him gave me a few seconds to take in Kroll without being obvious. He was seated gazing out the window and was, as one would expect, much the way he had been described. He was dressed in a leather motorcycle jacket. He had sandy colored, very neatly cut hair. And he looked deceptively soft, at least a trifle out of shape. Just knowing that we had an animal at hand who had tortured and brutally murdered a number of helpless young girls made my skin crawl.

Flaherty wrapped things up at the register, and the two of us sauntered out into the parking lot. If Kroll paid any attention to us at all we had no sense of it. But I caught a glimpse of his face as he talked with the unsuspecting waitress gracing her with a smile that looked like it was pasted on. When we reached the parking lot we continued to walk at a steady, unhurried pace.

"Do you think he paid any particular attention to us?" Flaherty asked when we reached our respective cars that were not too far from Kroll's SUV.

"I didn't think so!" I said.

"I know another way to bring the case to a head much quicker than the search!" Rich said. "We sit and wait till he comes out and blow his fucking brains out!"

CHAPTER SEVENTEEN

The splendor of the Coral Cliffs Townhomes far exceeded any reasonable expectations. The main building contained a multi-faceted maze of elegant suites in an Inca motif. Behind it an emerald green golf course languished in the shadow of a coral colored mountain. Our suite consisted of three bedrooms, a kitchen, dining and living rooms, and screened patios front and back. It was a home away from home with some added elegance!

"Now, all we have to worry about is if Kroll takes the bait and opts to transfer to Fredonia!" I said. "We will never find anything close to these accommodations in Page!"

"We're not giving him a choice," Lou said. "He's being temporarily assigned. Anyway, a guy with his proclivities will jump at the chance! For the lack of supervision if nothing else!"

Since we were all comfortably present we decided to turn it into a team meeting. Lou proceeded to spell out the shifts. We would be working from six to six. He and I would have the day shift and Jason and Rich would have nights. Once our quarry had gone to bed the night shift could work out of the motel suite and take turns sleeping while dressed and ready to go. When they got off at 6:00 am they would have until 1:00 pm to supplement their rest; all this to avoid the accumulative fatigue of steady nights over a period of weeks.

We were asked to keep an overnight suitcase in the car we were driving in case we found ourselves on our way out of town, unexpectedly.

Our week off would run from Thursday to Wednesday to keep the weekend pairings intact. He, Lou, would be the first out with me next. Jason would go third and Rich fourth. The relief man would take the fifth week before coming back on days.

"And we have to guard against overreacting," Lou continued. "We have to avoid, being seen by Kroll. If, for example, he is seen by you in a remote area checking him out you can alibi the first time away, but there would be no way you could do it a second. So you would be considered, for all intents and purposes, burned. We will have to go to the bullpen to find a replacement. If we are two in a car and it is necessary to check him out in some remote area, consider dropping your partner out of the car so we don't burn two at once. Is everyone clear on all of this?"

"Understood!" Jason said.

"Very clear!" added Richard.

"And," Lou added, "as harsh as it may sound there is a real possibility that Kroll's next victim will be the corpse that is going to convict him. In other words he might beat us to the punch in the killing but we will be too close at hand for him to get away with it. The timing is going to be very precarious!"

Then he looked over at me. "Do you have anything to add, Jim?"

"Just this!" I said. "It is most important that we not overreact! If, for example, he goes running off the beaten path and we are not sure he has anyone with him, it would be wise to wait and check out the area after he leaves. If he surprises us with a corpse we can depend on the fact that he will be back in his room at night! It is a harsh thing to say but we are already resigned to the fact that we may be faced with one more victim!"

It was not a welcomed realization and it brought on some somber nods!"

"You ought to plan on getting some clothes tomorrow," Lou said to me, in an abrupt change of pace. "It will be blue jeans for the most part. And you will need a couple of jackets, one light and one heavy to cover the hardware."

"If you don't know the weather," Jason said. "The winters are pretty mild. And because it's so dry in the desert 35 degrees will feel like 60 in Florida. It's at night that the cold weather really socks in and you can feel it. The desert doesn't hold the heat of the day!"

"What about snow?" I asked.

"We get some here and there, especially in January, but most of the time it is melted by evening." Jason said. "But Lou is right. Get some long sleeve cowboy shirts and jeans. A couple of jackets and you will be all set!"

It was Doran who spoke next. "What do you guys think about the recommendation of waiting a week before we slap on the transmitter?"

"Well he is probably going to be using the patrol car for his comings and goings until the weekend anyway," I said. "Why don't we figure on attaching it on Thursday night. Or rather Friday morning!"

"What about the motorcycle?" Flaherty asked. "What are we going to do about that?"

"Well," said Jason, "we always have the cell phone to monitor him!"

"If he was anyone but a cop," Lou said. "Most of us

know that the phone is a honing device. And, while he is flexible with his hours the department requires him to keep his cell phone handy in case he is needed. If he goes beyond recall, roughly more than three hours away, he has to let them know. The time when we are going to have to worry is when he turns it off! We have to hope, as terrible as it sounds, that his fetish has more elements than just an abrupt killing so we aren't without the opportunity to intervene!"

For several minutes we were each lost in our own somber thoughts! "I'll tell you what," Lou suddenly said brightly, "this might be the only time the four of us can sit down to dinner together, so why don't we ask Jason for a recommendation!"

"Houston's Trails End!" Bridges said without hesitation. "There are a lot of good restaurants in Kanab but the Trails is a steak house and I don't know about you, but I am in the mood for a nice thick steak!"

The mood at dinner that night was particularly festive. We knocked off a couple of bottles of fine wine and everything was upbeat until it started to get close to ten. Even though no one said it, the atmosphere began to weaken with the realization that we had not heard from Major Sawyer concerning whether or not Kroll had taken the bait! If we were going to have to spend a couple of months on this venture we were all hoping it would be at the Coral Cliffs, and it had begun to look like there was a chance we would have to move! The one problem with not allowing Lieutenant Gray into the loop is that if Kroll had any good reason for resisting the assignment, the lieutenant might well unwittingly assign someone else.

Just as Doran was signing the check his phone rang and we all held our collective breaths. But Lou was smiling and nodding as he listened and raised his thumb to let us know. We had all we could do to hold back a loud cheer.

"Well, guys," Lou said as he put his phone back in its holster, "he jumped all over the chance to move his act to Fredonia just like we thought! They gave him tomorrow off to pack and make the trip!"

That night I heard coyotes howl for the first time since I had come west. And howl they did from somewhere up there on those coral colored cliffs. They wailed for half the night! But, buried in blankets against the cold, it was a comforting sound and I had no trouble falling asleep in the midst of it.

CHAPTER EIGHTEEN

The office of the Grand Canyon Motel, assigned to be John Kroll's cozy home away from home, was a typical western ranch house more suited to a three hundred acre spread. A low-slung wood fence fronted it and it had a wagon wheel attached to its sign. Its units were a series of cabins that matched the motif. And it was conveniently located on the highway just south of what would be have to be called the center of town.

At 2:30 pm, Doran and I were seated in the green, non-intrusive older model Plymouth Neon he had brought us from the Las Vegas car pool. We had positioned ourselves about one hundred yards north of a bakery that was located just opposite the parking lot of the motel. And our GPS receiver was turned to channel three where we could see the circle surrounding the radio tower in Kanab gradually shrinking along Alternate 89. By our reckoning Kroll was less than ten minutes away.

In reality there was no point in being there at all but, while I had a previous sighting of Kroll, Lou, admittedly, felt compelled to lay eyes on this murderer as long as it was without risk. We knew that during the weeks ahead he would be primarily a blip on a screen and that, until we had sufficient cause to slap the cuffs on him, we likely would never even hear his voice. But it was the beginning and we both felt we needed to assess our prey.

We had spent the better part of the day canvassing the town of Fredonia, looking for places where we could sit in parked cars without drawing attention and for any likely dumping sites for annoying corpses.

At one point at the eastern end of Pratt Street we found an unpaved continuation that eventually led us to through an old abandoned logging area where new trees were well on the way to replacing the old. The road led to a dead end in front of a sprawling lake created by a remarkably engineered beaver dam; a lake populated with a battery of half-submerged white barked, leafless trees. Birds of every type abounded, benefiting from the natural advantages of a lake bequeathed from a less benevolent creek. It was a perfect example of the laws of nature at work.

"A good place to dump a body!" Doran said, "Who would ever have reason to come down here to catch you in the act!"

As if to confirm the impression, we both left the car and walked down to the dam to inspect it at closer range, only to be inundated by intense swarms of mosquitoes that viciously attacked what little we offered in the way of exposed flesh. We were both wearing lightweight jackets over our newly acquired long sleeve western shirts and jeans and had to raise them to cover our faces in the mad dash back to the car.

"This would be the perfect place to dump a body," Lou said once we were safely back inside the car. "Although you would have to dress like a Ninja to manage it. The neat thing about it is that the mosquitoes would have the victim stripped to the bone in a matter of minutes."

About 12:20 pm, as we scoured the city with one eye on the receiver, the cell phone circle surrounding the tower in Page began to expand along the highway. And in about twenty minutes it vanished as Kroll entered the dead space between towers. We found several places suitable for a sitting surveillance but none more useful or obvious than the Canyon itself for dumping a corpse.

Our new swingman, Glen Daniels, was also due that

afternoon bringing with him the fourth car. All of them would carry Utah license tags that were registered to a fictitious company in St. George.

"You know before this is through," Lou said, "you will get to know John Kroll like a book. It will be like an unhappy visit to an insane asylum. My first assignment, fresh out of Quantico, was the Dorothea Puente case. The Sacramento Police had just dug up seven bodies in her rose garden! Do you remember that one at all?"

"Vaguely," I said.

"Well the Sacramento P.D. started getting an unusual number of concerned parties checking in with them to find out why their fathers and uncles suddenly disappeared and the common denominator seemed to be the Puentes' boarding house. In checking further they found out that the government was still sending checks to these missing people at Puentes address. It became obvious what was going on. They took a look around the house and checked the basement before settling on the rose garden out back. Maybe the roses appeared uniquely nitrogen rich.

"Anyway, with a little digging they turned up the bones of seven victims. Another boarder turned up floating in a lake and still another was never found. Nine of them in all and there could have been more.

"I guess the point is that once you saw her you couldn't take your eyes off her. I pretty much just listened while two detectives attempted to elicit some useful information and saw how she handled herself. She was one tough cookie in a grandmother's skin. She was the consummate sociopath if there ever was one! But there was no question, now that you mention it, that she had all her marbles and then some. She knew the difference between right and wrong it's just that she didn't give a crap about it.

"And her life had been a mess from the very beginning. Married four times. Busted for running a whorehouse early on. Did five years for forgery! And as she sat there during that interview she could envision the gas chamber without batting an eye. I've seen a lot of hardened criminals in my career since then but none tougher than old Dorothy!"

"Do you think she could have passed a psychological?" I asked.

"It wouldn't exactly surprise me! She should have come off as cold, calculating and sociopathic, but not necessarily psychotic!"

Bridges's Ford Explorer patrol car had appeared on Main Street, briefly stopped, as it waited to turn into the parking lot of the motel! With an almost impeccable timing one of the two cars he had to wait on was a gold Mercedes SUV, pulling a small trailer with a motorcycle. We both made sure there were no passing vehicles on Main Street before raising our binoculars. I could see both parties emerge and Jason help Kroll to disengage his trailer and run it off to one corner of the parking lot and secure it to a tree. Then they both got into the patrol car and wheeled out to head north right on past us.

At that moment my phone jangled and it was Captain Abrams calling from Fort Lauderdale.

"Well the idiot finally fucked up," he said in that familiar baritone. "We have our body!"

"Oh, no!" I said, my heart sinking like a stone.

"Blocker is out at Executive Airport now waiting for the pilot. They are on the way up to Marion County to get the autopsy report and check the crime scene."

"It's definitely Caroline?" I asked.

126

"They've had her body since Tuesday," he said. "Or I should say most of her body parts, because he hacked her to pieces!"

"Oh, no!" I repeated. "That beautiful girl!"

"So far they did the teeth and called you on your cell, which of course was on top of your desk. The DNA will take a few more days."

"Where did they find her exactly? Marion County is Ocala isn't it?"

"In the Ocala National Forest. About 200 yards off a hiking trail. Some animal dragged a forearm out to the trail. If he had left her intact there's a good chance that no one would have found her. And he didn't have to do it, either! It isn't like he was smuggling a body out of a hotel in a suitcase. He did it right there at the scene. He did it strictly for kicks."

"Have you told Lee about it yet?"

"I've sent Betty Sullivan over to his house to break it to him and the mother. She has the expertise to do it as best it can be done!" And as an afterthought, "Where is the asshole now?"

I almost said he was just taking over the patrol car and caught myself in time. No one had been told our suspect was law enforcement. "He is back in town and we have him under surveillance as we speak.

"Well, do your level best to manufacture a reason to shoot the bastard!"

CHAPTER NINETEEN

We switched our channel to one and picked up the patrol car as it went to the north end of town, to Cowboy Drive where Jason Bridges lived. The cursor remained at the house for around thirty minutes before we watched it start up and head north on Main Street into Kanab. It came to a stop on East 300 Street. We rolled into town a good fifteen minutes after him and passed the patrol car, still parked in the heart of the commercial district. We switched to channel three and it indicated that he was physically located close to the car. We went around the block and found a parking spot where we could keep an eye on the car.

"My guess is he is in the barber shop," Lou said. "He's getting a haircut! Which reminds me….!"

I looked at Lou's abbreviated hairstyle and if he needed a haircut it wasn't apparent to me. I thought about Captain Abrams and the haircuts that were running down far too fast! An hour passed by and the car never moved, nor did we see any sign of Kroll.

"If he's in the barber shop he must be getting the works!" Lou said. "Maybe we should start looking for a guy with a shaved head!"

"It's his buddy!" I said, suddenly remembering Debbie Whitmore's telling us about his one friend.

"His buddy?" Lou asked. "The barber!"

"They go motorcycling together on weekends!" I said.

Another thirty minutes and we saw him emerge from

the shop and stand there with the barber while he locked the front door. They had a brief conversation on the street before Kroll went back to his car.

"He must have been with that guy for almost two hours." Lou said. "He has to be a really close friend!"

As the patrol car left we drove ahead to where we could see the front of the building with a barber's pole and lettering that spelled out "Joey's Barber Shop"!

"The name is Rizzo," I said, remembering the last name.

It was nearly six and time to change shifts so we headed back to the Coral Cliffs. The cursor was now parked at 332 W 300 Street.

"It's going to take us a little while to figure out the street numbering system in Kanab," Lou said. "It is all over the place!"

When we got back to the Cliffs the swingman, Glen Daniels, had arrived and was there to greet us at the door. He turned out to be even larger than Allen, in his early twenties, with blonde Nordic looks and a row of ivories that were positively incandescent. If the car he brought to town was suitably unobtrusive the same could not be said of him.

"He's one of our motor cops." Sawyer had told Doran, "with no tactical experience. But he is easy to get along with, does what he is told and knows how to bury a body!"

Daniels handed Doran his extra car keys and the latter handed us each one to add to our rings.

I left it to Lou to tell the team that we now had a corpse to add to the case and the reaction was everything one would expect. Bridges's brown eyes turned to stone.

"I'm glad I didn't know this earlier," he said quietly. 'I might not have been able to carry it off! Do you know if she was alive when they got to the forest?"

"We don't know that yet!" I answered. "But the hacking took place at the scene from all appearances and the hatchet was tossed a few feet away!"

"Maybe it was just my knowing what I didn't know before," Bridges said, "but today he really sccmcd crccpy to me. His handshake was like a dead fish! He felt like a corpse himself!"

"Well," said Lou, for the most part he is going to be a blip on a screen to us. What we are going to have to do is figure out his patterns. His routine! And be alert for deviations. Occasionally it will cause us to make a run on by wherever he is. For the most part, thanks to the modern technologies, we will be operating well out of his line of sight! And vice versa!"

"It is going to be different when we get to Las Vegas, though!" I said. "We are probably going to have to keep a closer eye on him. We are going to have to figure out how he works! How he makes his contacts!"

"So far he seems to be getting rid of at least a few girls he already knew!" Flaherty said.

"We are going to have to learn to anticipate!" Lou added. "If we are going to protect his next would-be victim we are going to have to see things develop before they actually do! Tell me, Jason, what do you know about Joey the barber."

"Well I don't know him at all," Jason said. "He's not my barber! But I did ask a female deputy about him!"

"And?"

"She told me that Rizzo is the kind of a guy who has an orgasm every time he handles a gun! He should be the NRA's Man of the Year! He's always bugging the Kane County deputies about using their range! And he likes to go out to a canal by Stagger Mountain Road to shoot targets! Now if you wanted to tell me that he was holding the lantern while Kroll was chopping up his victims I wouldn't be a bit surprised!"

"No, nothing like that!" Lou said. "Guys like Kroll work alone! There are only about 24 psychos like Kroll operating at any one time in the entire country and the odds that two of them could come together would be pretty steep!"

"Has it ever happened that you know of?" Flaherty asked.

"Once that I know of!" Lou said. "But the odds are heavily against it!

CHAPTER TWENTY

At the outset of our investigation of the murder of Caroline Albright the Bureau did a financial on Kroll. We wanted to track his vacation to prove that he was in Fort Lauderdale on October 17th. We learned that Kroll had, prior to his vacation, taken $4,000.00 dollars in cash from his bank in Flagstaff and refrained from using credit cards during the two weeks of his vacation, with two curious exceptions. On the 11th and the 24th of October he stayed at a Motel Six in Douglas, Arizona. A check of the map showed that the border town of Douglas was almost a hundred miles south of the natural highway east, Route #10. It was interesting to note, too, that at the conclusion of that vacation there was no cash re-deposit of any remaining balance.

"He covered his tracks completely by paying for everything with cash. At this point there is no sure way to prove that he ever got to Fort Lauderdale!" Lou said.

It was a terrible temptation not to lay the cards on the table, go for the search warrants and take our chances, especially with the prospect that the Mercedes van might well cough up some vital DNA in the form of at least a few of Caroline's blonde tresses. Instead we threw ourselves full boar into the longer plan of waiting him out.

During the weekdays that followed John Kroll fell, as no cop is trained to do, into a highly predictable pattern that made tracking his comings and goings about as difficult as a tap-in putt. It was the weekends that offered him his best opportunities to howl, however, and, given the theory that the killing urge welled up in cycles, the anxiety level rose progressively each succeeding Saturday. But the weekends, oddly, came and went without worry. Tracking him became like tailing the pope.

From Monday through Friday Kroll would emerge from his motel room at 8:00 am and have breakfast at Louie's. Then he would head out east on Alternate 89 and run traffic. He liked to run traffic! He would, in this the off-season, make around ten stops per day and write two to three citations. He would, dutifully, call in all of his stops; cars and license tags and properly advise his return to service.

His ticket production dwarfed anything produced by Jason Bridges, understandably, since the latter, after twenty-five years, was personally acquainted with half the people in both towns. Kroll's revenue producing, however, made his supervisor, the unsuspecting Lieutenant Gray, in a stressed economy, delirious!

There would be lunch up at Jacob's Lake and then he would take a run through town and out to the airport where he would spend another hour with traffic on the north end of town before calling it a day. About half his late afternoons were spent hanging around Joey Rizzo's barbershop. The rest of the time he would return to the motel and, we guessed, work on his computer or watch "Days of Our Live", there was no way to know for sure!

On the weekends our alert levels went into a higher gear. "Moving Day" is what Bridges called Fridays but for weeks there wasn't anything to get excited about. For a supposed recluse, Kroll fell in with a small motorcycling group that included his buddy, Rizzo, another guy and another couple with her on the back. They would convene on Saturdays at the Sinclair station across from the town hall and head out in any of four directions.

On the first Saturday Daniels and I saw the four bikes head north toward Kanab and could just as well let them go for the day. If there was the slightest possibility that Kroll had one ally in his extra-curricular endeavors, four would be out of the question! For lack of anything else to do, however, we followed along at an unseen distance with an eye on the cell phone blip, through the truly humbling canyons of the Zion National Park until we emerged in the gallant little town of Hurricane where we could see the four bikes parked outside the "Hurricane Inn".

We got ourselves hamburgers at McDonald's and parked where we could see the other restaurant where they were probably drinking and shooting snooker pool. It was two and a half hours before they all came out to don their helmets and kick start the bikes. They swept past us and on down Route 389, the alternate route back to Fredonia. Daniels and I continued to follow past the two wooden bridges that led to Colorado City and on down the road to Fredonia.

Kroll spent most of his Sundays fishing the Kanab Creek with or without the company of his buddy Rizzo. Somehow we got the idea that Joey's wife begrudged the amount of time Joey spent with Kroll because she never joined them or invited her husband's pal to dinner.

I was off the next week and toyed with the idea of flying back to Fort Lauderdale but couldn't bring myself to get that far away. I hung around on Saturday morning hitting balls at the golf course driving range. But at the appointed hour of 8:00 am the bikers convened again and this time they opted to take the northern route right past the golf course on the way to Lake Powell. I could see them as they roared on by.

I hung around Sunday, played golf on Monday and then headed to Las Vegas for two days doing more sightseeing than gambling at various points along the strip.

During the weeks that followed we got to see a lot of that corner of the west and it was amazing how much there was to see. Kanab is famous for the filming of western movies. The epic "Western Union" was filmed there, as well as most of the "Gunsmoke" television series. As a tourist attraction the area, in and around Kanab was, without a doubt, a truly underappreciated gem.

Kroll had another shining moment on the job when two hikers, up near the north rim of the canyon, got separated from their group and failed to return to the hotel at night. Using his guide instincts Kroll found them the following day. Major Sawyer called Lou to tell him that the department was awarding Kroll with a commendation and that his unsuspecting lieutenant was gushing over the job he was doing.

On the Sunday before Thanksgiving Kroll broke the routine by taking a trip in his van back to the motor home at Cameron Station. After spending the better part of an hour inside the trailer he surprised us by heading on up the road to Flagstaff. We followed along at the usual unseen distance and saw the cursor move into the downtown area and park on Aspen Avenue at the intersection of San Francisco Street. We followed east on Santa Fe Avenue past the railroad station and turned on San Francisco Street. It was a one-way north. When we got to Aspen it was a one-way east so we had to go around the block until we found a parking spot on the left side of Aspen right in front of Babbitt Brothers Sporting Goods. We had a view of the gold Mercedes on the opposite side of the street about a half block ahead of us. Lou switched to the cell phone channel and could see that Kroll was at that moment proceeding east on Santa Fe, a long block south of where we were sitting.

We kicked around the thought of one of us hoofing it down to Santa Fe to see if we could figure out what he was doing but finally opted to stay put.

It wasn't long before the cell phone cursor was moving back west to San Francisco Street and proceeding north in our direction. In a few minutes he came around the corner, empty handed, got into his car and took off heading east to Agassiz where he could turn south back to Santa Fe and on out of town.

With Lou behind the wheel we followed the same route and after turning back west on Santa Fe I kept my eyes trained on the row of stores trying to figure out which one he might have gone into and for what reason. It was like looking for a needle in a haystack. The row of small single story shops had a distinctly western motif about them; and I had Lou slow down while I noted the names. Among the stores were a Pony Express Postal, a Grand Canyon Café, a Galaxy Saddle and Leather Shop, and a Wildwest Trader's; nothing that jumped out to account for a fifteen-minute investment of Kroll's time.

By this time our quarry was well along Route #89 on the way back to Fredonia.

Lou took the fact that he was not going to spend Thanksgiving with his family without complaint but we got caught by surprise on the day before. In the morning we were parked out by the airport waiting for the Kroll's patrol car to begin the day. It got to be 9:00 am before we checked the cell phone on channel three and there was no cursor at all. We went to channel two and could see that the Mercedes was traveling 389 west and was, by that time, halfway to Colorado City. We both surmised that, with permission from Page, he was on his way to visit his mother in Kingman with his cell phone turned off. And we were right!

At 1:00 PM that afternoon, after letting them sleep, we notified Bridges that he and Flaherty had some traveling to do and Lou and I rolled into Kingman around 3:00 in the afternoon. We got to touch base with Peterson and we had

Thanksgiving dinner the next day with Roy and his truly beautiful wife, Marge.

When Kroll left town on Friday there was the thought that he would head for Las Vegas for the rest of the weekend. But, instead, he went straight around the lake and back to Fredonia. Apparently it was part of the trade-off that he work that weekend

On Friday, December 4th, we had our first incident of major concern. Lou was on vacation and I was partnered with Glen Daniels and we were coming to the end of another uneventful shift. As we were turned in the direction of the motel I was watching the cursor of the Explorer patrol car move into and through the commercial district of Kanab. On his way to dinner we thought.

But the car continued on out into the northwest residential district and made its way down to a street called West Rawhide Drive.

"He must be meeting with one of his motorcycle pals," I said. "For a guy who is supposed to be reclusive he is becoming more gregarious by the day!"

My phone rang and it was Bridges. "We are on duty and we see the patrol car is parked on Rawhide Drive. Anyway we got it!"

After we hung up I turned to Glen and told him that I thought we ought to check out whom Kroll is picking up or, as the case may be, visiting for dinner. We drove on out to the area in question which was located at the end of some residential streets where the houses were really spaced well apart. We drove on by the comfortable ranch style, with the patrol car in front, and on around the bend where we found a place to park away from any other house. Although the patrol car was faced west it seemed likely that, if he was going to head back to town he would turn around and head back east.

In a few minutes the cursor began to move, looped around and began coming our way. We let it pass and there was enough daylight to see that there was a black haired female in the passenger seat. We waited until it was out of sight and began to follow at a distance using the GPS to show us the way.

We continued on into town and right on to Center Street headed east. Kroll parked on Center Street directly across from Houston's Trail's End and the two were just preparing to cross the street as we went on by. I had Daniels keep his eyes ahead while I took a furtive look at Kroll's companion. She was very young looking, quite possibly not even twenty and extremely attractive. She was wearing a white miniskirt that barely made it to the knees giving emphasis to a long, leggy gait. He was dressed in a conforming business suit. At the same time we saw Bridges's tan Chevy parked on the restaurant side of the street.

The phone rang and it was Bridges. "We need to talk!"

"Let's meet in the parking lot of the Four Seasons," I suggested. It was only a block away.

The four of us piled out of our cars and went inside!

"You know what I think," Bridges said when we had piled into a booth. "I think I ought to call up my wife and have her and I go over to the Trails for dinner. I mean right now. Naturally we will see Kroll and the obvious next step is to say hello and get introduced to the lovely lady. It would put the kibosh on any plans he might have to knock her off!"

"She's not in any danger, Jason," I said. "Not now! Not when he is seen with her in public! Maybe well on down the road if she ever decides to dump him! But she is okay for now! Trust me!"

"I guess you are right," Jason said, after a little thinking.

"But we need to get her identification for future reference!" I said. "Her car is inside a closed garage at home so we will have to wait until she is on the streets to get her tag number!"

"I can run the address through the utilities on Monday," Jason said.

"And you will probably get her parents names," I said. "The girl is very young!"

"I wonder where he met her," Jason said.

"My bet is that he stopped her in traffic," Flaherty said. "According to our logs he doesn't seem to have had any calls for service that would have brought them together!"

Allen and Flaherty settled for coffee and left early while Glen and I remained to have dinner. When we got to the car we checked our GPS and we could see that the car was on its way back to the house on Rawhide Drive. Case closed for the moment at least.

The next day the motorcycles convened as usual at the Sinclair station and left with a roar along the southern route to Page.

CHAPTER TWENTY-ONE

On the morning of Friday, December 18th, just a week before Christmas, Lou and I went outside to find a powdery snow falling, covering the cars with a light film. It was the first time I had seen snow in twenty years.

"Enjoy it while you can," Lou said, "because it will all be gone with the rising sun!"

And it was!

But there was another deviation from the normal routine.

Kroll returned to the Grand Canyon Motel immediately after lunch. On a hunch I drove the Neon to our spot north of the bakery and in thirty minutes we saw Kroll emerge, out of uniform, carrying two suitcases that he tossed into the back of the Mercedes. He left town via the southern route to Las Vegas.

We fell into a following pattern, well back and out of sight. Lou called Flaherty to tell him that they had some traveling to do and to bring Bridges who was on his week off.

It wasn't until we passed the turnoff to Boulder City and knew that Kroll was not headed to his mother's that we called Ken Allen to make reservations for four of us somewhere in town. Lou would be spending the night at home. At 5:00 pm we rolled into North Las Vegas about five miles behind the Mercedes. If it was accurate to say that Christmas lights abounded they made no noticeable impact upon the lighting already in place.

We followed Kroll's cursor to the parking lot of the Fremont Hotel in the old downtown. I tooled into the parking lot of Fitzgerald's a block away. Thirty minutes later, the rest of our crew rolled in.

We all convened outside of our car and it fell to Lou to set the plan!

"This could be it, guys," he said. "You can be sure that if this was a fun trip for him he would have invited his cute, little squeeze!" We had identified her as Ann Boyle and her age as nineteen.

"I don't know if you checked or not," Flaherty said, "but his cell phone is also turned off!"

"That confirms it," Lou said. "The deal with the department is that he remain on call up to 200 miles away. Not that he can respond to trouble, but he remains available for transporting a prisoner or investigating an incident after the fact. If he goes home to see mama for example he is supposed to advise communications and they have to send a deputy up from Page if needed."

"So he's probably told them he is gone to Kingman for the weekend," I said.

"Exactly!" Lou said. "As far as the cell phone is concerned it is no real problem as long as we have the car bugged. He is not likely to carry some girl piggy back out of town!"

"Do we need to do visuals on him at all?" Bridges asked.

"Well it might tell us how he operates and it might tell us who his next victim is! But on the other hand it is not worth any risk of being detected. So we will follow him loosely with a variety of faces, using the phones to keep us in sync! We will have Bridges and Flaherty man a two-man post to quicken the communications. I will use Jason as my base and Glen and Jim use Richard. Jason, you drive your car to the Fremont parking lot and put the Mercedes under surveillance. We are going to have to know if Kroll is alone when he moves the car.

"Allen is on his way here and should be arriving any minute. He will also use Jason as his base. All we have to do is spread out and walk around in the hope of spotting him. But if you do eyeball him play it safe. Don't be afraid to lose him. It's 7:00 o'clock so go have dinner. Jim you have yours at the Golden Gate at the end of the street, Glen you have yours at Fitzgerald's and I will hang around the Fremont. When Allen gets here we will send him to the Nugget. Keep in touch."

Unhurried, I took the long stroll down Fremont Street where the canopy lights were already turned on. If you've never seen it, in a miracle of imagination, the glaring lights under the canopy along Fremont turn the midnight hours into high noon! Christmas songs were blaring from loudspeakers along the way, in an almost futile attempt to inject some holiday spirit into an environment where people had their minds on other interests.

In a recovering economy there seemed to be as many people circulating as the street could accommodate, a fact that would make it a lot easier to tag along with Kroll if we were to ever find him. The phone rang and it was Flaherty with the latest report.

Kroll had gotten into his car alone and was driving on Carson Avenue westbound toward Main Street that was in my direction but one block over. I kept walking even though I was getting further from my own transportation and there was a good chance that Kroll was headed for the Strip. Flaherty remained on the line with me until we were able to ascertain where the guy was headed.

To our surprise he turned north on Main Street and pulled into the parking lot just across from the Plaza, about a hundred yards in front of where I was walking. I had just passed the Golden Gate Hotel when I saw him crossing Main Street still dressed the way we had seen him earlier, in a blue plaid western shirt and jeans. However, he was now wearing a baseball cap and sunglasses. There was a lot of panther in the way he moved and his lengthy stride forced me to quicken my pace to maintain the distance between us.

Kroll sauntered under the Plaza Marquee in the direction of the Greyhound bus station without looking around or showing any concern that he might be followed. He pushed through the glass doors with the same lack of suspicion. I hit the doors about five minutes later and headed straight for the newsstand to get a paper without looking right or left. I took a seat and opened the paper before checking the house.

Kroll had taken a seat at the far end of the room next to a very attractive girl who appeared to be unaccompanied. She also appeared to be very young, probably college age.

Kroll was smiling and the girl was smiling as he talked to her but she would occasionally shake her head. At one point he showed her his wallet identification and she studied it before shaking her head some more. He smoothly removed his sunglasses so that she could see his eyes and, instinctively, I scanned the wall for cameras. There was only one non-oscillating camera trained on the ticket window and I was sure that Kroll had made himself aware of that!

The public address began to announce that the bus for Los Angeles was now boarding and I could see the girl stand up still smiling and pick up her suitcase. Kroll took the suitcase from her and walked with her out of the west exit and across to the bay where the bus was standing and people were depositing their suitcases on the island to be put on board.

I stood up and went to the window where I could see the girl board the bus while giving him a friendly little wave. With a shrug of his shoulders he turned away from the bus and headed back toward the parking lot where his car was parked.

My phone rang and it was Allen. He had finally arrived and was in the parking lot where Kroll was headed along with Daniels. I told them to evaporate and I would join them as soon as Kroll drove off. Then I went to the ticket window and got a bus schedule, noting that there were three Los Angeles bound buses per day, including weekends. At ten, four and eight!

As soon as the gold Mercedes left the parking lot I made my way across the street to where both Allen and Daniels were standing outside his Crown Victoria.

"What was he doing in the bus station?" Ken wanted to know.

"Well, if sign language means anything at all, he was trying to talk a pretty young lady out of taking the bus. My guess is that he told her he was driving to Los Angeles and wanted some company."

"That's a pretty good M.O.," Ken said. "It will be interesting to see if he tries that again tomorrow!"

"I think he probably will!" I said, waving the bus schedule at him before putting it away.

Right on schedule our command vehicle made a turn on Main Street and headed south toward the Strip. The three of us piled into Allen's county car and headed off in the same direction. We had no GPS with us so we had to keep up with Bridges and Flaherty.

Ten minutes later Flaherty was on my phone again. "He's turning into the north side parking lot of the Luxor!" he said. "Maybe he's going to turn his next girl into a mummy!" Then after a pause he added, "Lou wants you to park on the south side and wait for instructions."

While we sat looking at the pyramid shaped Luxor Allen observed. "You know it's funny about the hotel themes. They can have a New York skyline or an Egyptian pyramid, or whatever. As soon as you step into the main room every one of them looks the same! A sea of slots, roulette wheels and green felt tables. Except for maybe Caesar's Palace where you have a bunch of fountains and people running around in togas!"

"The same thing with the Christmas decorations," Daniels said. "There is almost no way they can create the mood. It is almost an exercise in futility!"

Daniels's phone rang and it was Lou giving him the first shot at going inside to see what our guy was up to. It was nearly nine o'clock.

"Do you think it might have been a good idea for one of us to jump on that bus and find out what Kroll was telling her?" Allen asked when we were alone.

"I thought about it for a second or two," I said. "But the truth is that she probably wasn't going to tell us anything more than we were able to surmise! The risk wasn't worth the effort!"

In a little while Flaherty called to tell us that Kroll was at the black jack table gambling and doing a lot of looking around. A while later we got another update! Kroll had become part of the onlookers at one of the crap tables but wasn't making any bets.

At ten o'clock Daniels came out to climb into our car. Lou had replaced him.

An hour later one of the cocktail waitresses exited the south entrance still dressed in a G-string and see through pantaloons and navigated the aisles between the parked cars on the way to her own. Lo and behold Kroll appeared a comfortable distance behind her and timed it so that by the time her black Miata was backing out he was in a perfect position to make note of her license plate. Then he turned around and headed back for the building. A few minutes after that Flaherty announced that the Mercedes was out on the Strip and headed back to the Fremont Hotel.

That night Flaherty drew the assignment of staying up with the GPS while the rest of us slept until seven.

CHAPTER TWENTY-TWO

On Saturday morning I was the first one down to the buffet breakfast, having sent Flaherty to bed by taking over the GPS. It was amazing how bustling the room was at 8:00. In the next half hour our team materialized one at a time and with people pressing in on all sides there didn't seem to be any way to discuss business. So we busied ourselves with eating in relative silence.

A cute little waitress went around the table filling our cups with coffee, while apologizing for the slowness of service.

"We are a little shorthanded this morning," she explained, "because one of our waiters won a million dollars last night playing the one dollar slots. It's just so amazing to be a hard working slob one day and a millionaire the next! But, on the other hand, it happens all the time! Why can't it happen to me?"

This caused Allen to raise his head with a wry smile. As soon as she was out of earshot he said, "Can you believe that? She's shilling!"

I caught it, too. "How do you suppose she gets compensated for that?" I asked.

"It's just a case of turning a negative into a positive," he said. "They are probably shorthanded and this is a way of making people happier about the delays! The patron's all want to believe that someone can beat the system. It plays right into their fantasies!"

Lou, coming from home, was the last to arrive and settled for coffee on the arm. "Well the party is on for sure," he said quietly. "But don't expect things to go down today necessarily! Our cat is more than willing to play with the mouse for as long as it takes. Or mice, as the case may be! The game is just as important to him as the kill and that makes him very patient. He probably gets a charge out of just knowing that the girl he has his eyes on has her very life in his hands! It is, for him, like playing God!"

He stopped talking as some people settled at a table next to ours. Then he leaned forward and in a voice just beyond a whisper said, "We are going to shuffle things up a bit! We are without Flaherty so Jason and I will drive the Plymouth. The rest of you take the Chevy. You my as well sit down at the Golden Gate as well as anywhere since we expect him to check out the bus terminal at ten. Jason and I will sit on the SUV! Today we will avoid moving around on foot. Stay with the cars! There is no need to take any risks!"

Lou, like the rest of us was looking around for the girl with the coffee!

"They're a little shorthanded this morning," Ken said dryly.

"Don't tell me one of their waiters hit the dollar slots again!" Lou said. He'd heard it before!

"We need to save our faces as much as possible," Lou continued, "and you guys, if I may say so, are far too good looking not to get noticed! I keep asking for ordinary looking guys and look what they send me! So the focus has to be on the car! It's all about the car. Remember to top off your tanks at every opportunity and make sure you eat when the opportunity is there. In short keep everyone and everything fueled and ready!"

The girl showed up and we got coffee all around, and then headed off to do our constitutionals before convening at the cars.

At 9:30 Ken and I were parked across from the Plaza with Glen, who preferred to do the driving, behind the wheel, when my phone jangled. "He's alone!" Lou said, and hung up. There was no need for wasted breath.

We watched as the cursor left the Fremont parking lot and moved over to Carson Avenue before heading our way.

"It's almost eerie how we have this guy figured out!" Glen said.

"You do get that feeling after a while," Ken said

In a few minutes the Mercedes arrived and parked well away from us. Kroll emerged, dressed in his best western, another blue plaid shirt and jeans, and headed across Main Street toward the Plaza.

It wasn't until ten that he returned, ducking the traffic nimbly enough as he jogged back across Main. But instead of returning to his car he walked right past it and on toward the Golden Gate Casino. Fortunately he was one aisle over or else three guys in a car might have caught his attention. I called Lou to tell him.

"Stick with the plan and let him do his thing," he said. "Just keep an eye on the car!"

Ken volunteered to go over to the Plaza and get us more coffee and doughnuts and I went with him. Back in the car we settled in for the long haul. We took turns with the war stories for the next three hours, occasionally getting out to stretch and walk around a little. At noon Allen and Daniels left to grab some lunch and they elected to walk across the street to the Vegas Club in order to avoid accidentally

149

running into Kroll. When they returned I did the same. At 1:30 I had just returned when we saw Kroll coming around the outside of the Golden Gate and head for his car. When the Mercedes left the parking lot we never moved. We watched the icon turn back on to Carson and proceed past the first casino and pull into the Nugget parking lot next door. After only a stop of a few minutes the icon returned to Carson and headed back toward the Fremont. There was no need to call Lou since they had their own receiver. We decided to stay put.

"He may have picked someone up!" I said.

Sure enough he returned to the Fremont parking lot.

"He's back and he is talking with a female driver of a second car!" Lou told me on the phone. "Now he is going inside the hotel and she is still sitting in her car!"

After a short wait Kroll came out to his car carrying two small suitcases and tossed them in the back. Then the two cars pulled out and went back to Carson Avenue and were headed back our way. "He is following the girl," Lou told me on the phone. My guess is that they are headed for her place and she is going to pack a few things. He's got a live one!"

The Mercedes passed us in a few minutes and proceeded south toward the Strip. Glen backed the car up and we turned out on to the street to follow. The Plymouth, however, passed right in front of us and we fell in behind. Kroll drove south on the Strip to Flamingo where he hung a left. He went on over to Eastern Avenue before turning right.

"We are in the area of the university," Allen said. "Dollars to donuts the girl is a student who lives nearby!"

A block from the campus we could see the icon turn onto a side street and slow. Then stop! We were about three minutes behind him and as we came down the street we could see him climbing the front steps of an apartment house with a girl walking in front of him. We swept on by.

Glen drove around the block and found a parking space where we could see the Mercedes from about a hundred yards away. Bridges, who was driving the other car, opted to park a short distance away from the street and leave the observation to us.

It was nearly an hour before Kroll and the girl came out of the apartment building with him carrying her suitcase. They were going on a trip. I reported this to Lou. The girl looked from a distance to be around 20, possibly younger, attractive and dressed in a blouse and jeans.

Fortunately they decided to use the Mercedes and not her car. It would have sabotaged our entire pursuit but, at the same time, probably his plans as well. In a few minutes they were underway taking the first turn north. About the time Glen kicked it into gear and turned the corner the icon had come to a stop on Flamingo. Glen slowed us down but then decided on a drive by and we saw the Mercedes had pulled into an Exxon Station and Kroll was already getting out of the car. We went on ahead a few blocks before finding a place to park.

It took another ten minutes before the Mercedes was moving again passing us before it took the ramp to Route 515, but, surprisingly, it was headed north, not south toward Los Angeles. Glen took his time and we got onto the highway about five minutes later with the Plymouth directly behind us.

The icon ran along the expressway until it ended and slid on to Route 95, still headed north.

"Reno!" Ken said from the rear seat. "He has talked her

into going to Reno! And along the way they will pass right by Death Valley. That's the plan for sure. You can bet that girl is never going to see Reno today or tomorrow!"

I passed that along to Lou and he agreed that our alert level had undertaken a major jump.

"How long a drive is it to Reno?" Glen asked.

"I hope you realize that question is purely rhetorical," Ken answered. "Because they really aren't going there! But to answer your question it's over 400 miles. It's a good ten hours of driving! So he must have convinced her that they will be spending the night half way! Probably in Tonopah!"

And so it was as we ran beyond the shadows of the Spring Mountains and on across the bleak desert where the first town of any size would be Beatty, over three hours away! We would be skirting the Nellis Bombing and Gunnery Range, a vast barren expanse off to our right, larger in area than two of our states!

The amount of traffic along the highway was light to put it mildly and nearly all of what we saw was headed in the opposite direction and most of that was 18-wheelers. Once in a while we would overtake a beat up heap cautiously struggling to remain operable in the steaming heat.

We discovered early on that one of the peculiarities of a dry climate and a clear atmosphere is the eerie ability to see for miles. This meant that in order not to be seen by Kroll we had to hang back an unusual distance. Although Route 95 was the only road to Reno and there was not a lot of potential to leave in another direction we still felt that hours of following at a matching speed might trigger suspicion. So after gauging his speed to be 75 miles per hour, we dropped back out of sight and set our cruise control to match.

Bridges and Doran were traveling in our wake with

Jason behind the wheel.

An hour out we could see the cursor pass the intersection of Route 160 and I took a look at my watch in order to time our distance behind. Much to our surprise it took us another twenty minutes to reach the same intersection. In order to remain unsighted we were giving away twenty minutes, enough time for him to snuff the poor girl with some minor preliminaries.

Not good!

If Kroll got to Beatty twenty minutes ahead of us he could gas up, grab a couple of sandwiches be ready to get back on the road before we even got there. If we, on the other hand, overtook him and passed him he would have no reason to suspect he was being followed, we could get to Beatty ahead of him, gas up and grab sandwiches for all of us. And for all we knew Kroll could opt for a sit down meal, a sort of fattening the cat for the kill. That is, if his hormones weren't getting the best of him

It would mean running the risk of being stopped for speeding but we could all flash badges and give the trooper a quick explanation. The only way to communicate out there in the middle of nowhere was head to head so we had Ken, in the back seat, wave Bridges alongside and through lowered windows give them our plan. After getting the green light, Glen took us up to it 85 miles per hour and immediately the Mercedes came into view, a little gold speck far down the highway.

It took us nearly an hour of closing the distance to catch up to Kroll and as we went by I gave them the back of my head to look at while Daniels kept his eyes on the road. We left it to Allen to sneak a peek at the occupants from the back seat and he was able to affirm that, at least for the moment, the quarry was still sitting upright and looking calm!

As we began to pull away from the other car there was a sign announcing that Beatty was only 12 miles ahead. As soon as we built a lead we had to take it down as we reached the city limits. At just after 6:00 pm a small diner showed up on our right and Glen left the road and pulled to a stop. In a few minutes the Mercedes went on by headed to the center of town.

CHAPTER TWENTY-THREE

The township of Beatty, Nevada, popularly known as the gateway to Death Valley, was a major watering hole, strategically placed, along the highway between Reno and Las Vegas. It was a town of motels and restaurants catering to truckers and tourists with a handful of modest casinos along its Main Street.

Except for its main drag, there was an uncharted, rugged look about Beatty, a western informality completely without pretension. It was not a town of manicured lawns and leashed dogs. In short, the township of Beatty was really a throwback to a time when people weren't that bothered by what went on next door or down the block.

I dropped my partners at the diner and took over the wheel. The curser on the GPS had moved to South Second Street and hung a right on East Main. I slowly rolled out onto the highway and took off in the same direction.

I knew Kroll was going to have to stop. My own gas tank was one quarter full and the next gas was ninety miles away. But the cursor continued north until it finally pulled off the road to the left somewhere in the 900 block of West Main Street.

I made the same turn onto Main and went past a couple of Casinos, noting that there was a large, truck friendly gas station at the next intersection. Continuing on until I reached the point where the cursor had stalled I could see that Kroll's car was located in the parking lot of the Stagecoach Hotel and Casino. I found a parking spot and walked over to the main building to see if they had stopped to eat. There was a restaurant connected to the casino called Allen's Steak House and I stepped inside to look around. About midway I could see Kroll and the girl being handed menus and it was obvious that they would be there for a while.

My first stop was the gas station to top off the tank. Then it was back down the road to the diner where the other car had already arrived. Disengaging the monitor I went inside to join the group, which now included all five of us.

There was not a single doubt that this was going to be it. Kroll had to be back to work on Monday, at least as far as we knew, and he couldn't get much further removed from Fredonia than he was right now. We reasonably believed that Death Valley would be the critical destination and that the girl from Las Vegas would be history if we did not intervene at exactly the right moment.

By 7:45 we were positioned in the parking lot of the Sourdough Casino, with four of us huddled as though we were about to call the next play. Only Daniels remained inside a car with an eye on the monitor. It occurred to Lou to check our phones and see if any of them worked in Beatty. The only one that did was Daniels' Verizon.

"The question is probably moot anyway because none of them are going to work in Death Valley!" Lou said. "And, rest assured, that's where he is headed."

There were several minutes of quiet thought before Lou spoke up again. "We are going to gamble that he is going to take the time to play a game of cat and mouse with his victim before he lowers the boom!"

"I agree," Allen said. "To be blunt he is probably going to want to screw her while she is still alive!"

"It's refreshing to find someone with such a knack for delicate expression." Lou said dryly. "So we are going to give him some time before we close in. Ten minutes ought to be enough for him to get her tied or unconscious, or whatever it is he does!"

"What a risk!" Daniels said quietly. "I've got a sister her age!"

"It's a risk we have to take," Allen said. "But the odds are better than you would get at the tables around here!"

"There's one more thing," Lou said. "When we get him apprehended, let me do the talking. If we all start asking questions we can screw up the pattern. We have to remember that, as far as we know, he doesn't know we found the Albright girl's body!"

"He's moving!" Daniels said through the open window. "And he is coming our way!"

This sent us scrambling back inside our respective cars.

In a few minutes we could see the Mercedes pull into the gas station and Kroll get out to pump. Five minutes later he was out on the street and headed south on 374 toward Death Valley. We gave him a ten-minute lead before venturing out onto the highway. This time I was driving the following car.

The cursor had gone only a mile or so before it took an unexpected right on an unnamed street. When we got to the intersection in question there was a large billboard that announced our departure from Beatty, the imminent approach of Death Valley and an arrow indicating that the road Kroll had taken led to a ghost town. It was a paved road that swept along a string of low-rise mountains like an ominous highway to nowhere!

"Rhyolite!" Allen said suddenly, like it was a foreign language.

"What do you mean Rhyolite," I asked.

"It's the ghost town!" Ken said. "The son-of-a-bitch is going to snuff her in the middle of a ghost town!"

"Doesn't anyone live there at all?" I asked.

"Absolutely no one as far as I know! And at this hour there won't be any tourists either. They will probably have the place to themselves!"

"He's been here before!" I said.

"That would be my guess," Ken agreed, "or I would have expected him to head on into Death Valley. Maybe he's got some trees in there to tie her to and that offer a little concealment! He wouldn't find anything like that in the Valley!"

"And. for what it's worth," Glen said, "his car is about a half mile ahead and parked on the left side of the road!"

"We better stop!" I said, flashing my lights to signal the lead car before leaving the road.

Bridges stopped the lead car and put it in reverse, backing it up to where we were waiting. The three of us got out and walked forward to the other car.

"Has anybody been in this place before?" I asked.

"I have!" Lou said. "About five or six years ago! But I know a little about what it's like!"

"A lot of empty, dilapidated buildings?" Ken asked.

"Well, it's not like Jerome, if that's what you're thinking!" Lou said. "This town died before World War One! It was a frenzied gold rush town that petered out in a hurry.

This place is a wide-open field of brush and rocks about a mile long! There is a restored house made of beer bottles, a restored railroad station and a handful of shell structures that look like post-war Berlin! If this guy was in one of those skeleton buildings there would be no way to sneak up on him. They are all well separated from each other!"

"Are there any trees at all?" Ken asked.

"None that I can remember! It's all wide open! But you could slide inside one of the shells if there were enough walls still left standing, and be pretty much out of sight!"

"And the sun is already sinking," Jason said. "In an hour you won't be able to see your hand in front of your face!"

"What we are going to have to do is ride in at a leisurely pace like some late tourists," I said. "Maybe at twenty mile per hour! And when we get to where the car is we are going to have to suddenly punch it! We are going to have to storm the place!"

After a brief exchange of glances and no better idea Lou made the first move. He went to the rear of the Neon, popped the trunk and after a short shuffle came up with a vest that he put on securing the Velcro.

"Do any of you have vests with you?" he asked, invoking a shake of heads. "Because if he's killed the girl already he is certainly going to try to kill you!" He then produced a lightweight jacket with the large letters of FBI across the back. "Okay, then! I'll lead! Let's do it!"

159

CHAPTER TWENTY-FOUR

At 8:10 pm we rolled into what used to be the gold rush town of Rhyolite, one car behind the other, until we could see the four walled skeleton of a what used to be a relatively large one story stone building. It had a series of open windows all the way around and no roof. And we could barely see the nose of the Mercedes tucked up close against the rear of the building.

Jason was behind the wheel of Lou's car, which suddenly veered onto a dirt road that angled up to the left front of the building. I veered onto a nearer dirt road and then swung a right onto another road that led to the rear and brought us nose to nose with Kroll's van. We all bailed out and ran to the building with guns drawn and everyone picked their own window. The scene inside surpassed our most excessive anticipation.

A naked Kroll suddenly dropped to his knees to reach in the carry bag for what was likely a handgun, but thought better of it and leaned back while raising his hands to put them behind his neck. The girl was lying naked on her back a few feet away, squirming, while attempting to hold her legs tight enough to restrict us to the briefest glimpse of the tip of her pubic trail! Her handcuffed hands were tied to a padlocked chain that encircled the separation of two of the windows. Her breasts were unavoidably exposed and her mouth was duct taped. Her eyes looked wildly from us to Kroll and back to us.

"Down!" Allen shouted to the weirdly composed Kroll. "Flat on your stomach! Hands behind your head!"

Kroll did not move at first. He had seen Bridges and the expression on his face was something to¹ see. His eyes traveled from Jason to the windows that revealed his car realizing in an instant that his car had to be bugged.

Allen was the first one through the open door that separated the windows and, gun drawn down on Kroll repeated his order.

Kroll, finally, while keeping his hands behind his head, slowly proceeded to lie face down. "You guys are making a big mistake!" he said. "This whole thing is not what it looks like at all! It's a game! It's entirely consensual! This is a private matter between two adults!"

Allen could barely suppress a laugh. "It looks consensual!" he said. "Why would anyone ever think otherwise?"

He reached down and picked up the suitcase and a short riding crop that was lying on the floor where Kroll had dropped it. The crop was the type a jockey used, harmless enough, and capable of little more than stinging a willing subject, which caused us to wonder. Ken moved them out of reach.

By this time we were all inside with our guns re-holstered. Lou went immediately to the girl and taking his jacket off covered her below the waist. "A couple of you guys get their clothes from the car!" he ordered. Glen and Jason responded immediately as Lou unlocked the handcuffs, freeing her hands and arms. Then he knelt down to yank the tape from her mouth. "This may hurt a little, sweetheart," he said before ripping the tape in one swift motion.

The girl rolled to her knees, stood up with her back to us, and worked the jacket around to cover her exposed derriere, tying the arms in front of her. Her figure, at first

161

glance was flawless, and she had a pretty face to go with a healthy shock of auburn hair. She moved toward a corner of the room and with her back to us, turned her head to speak in a soft, somewhat embarrassed tone.

"John is telling the truth," she said. "This is not what it looks like! This is all.......consensual! A fantasy acted out!"

"That's what you think, sweetheart," Allen responded, but cut it short as Lou raised his hand.

"Let's get them dressed first."

Jason and Glen were back carrying clothes from the car, Jason hers and Glen his. For my part, having more than a few incidents in a long career of all hell suddenly breaking loose, I kept my focus on Kroll.

Glen let the boots fall to the floor and tossed the boxer shorts on the middle of Kroll's back. "Okay, Ace, let's put some clothes on!" he said.

Kroll got to his feet and slid his shorts on before catching his western style shirt. Before tossing the pants, Glen removed a wallet, a comb and some loose change.

"I'll take those," Ken said and stepped forward to collect them. He unzipped one of the side pouches in the carry bag and slid them inside.

Kroll had to sit on the floor to put on his boots. And it donned on me that she must have helped him remove them in the first place. It's difficult to do it alone.

"I really don't know what this is all about," Kroll said as he pulled up the boots. "But I think you guys are operating on very shaky grounds here and I have a right to know why you were following me!"

"Let's have you stay seated right where you are until we get this all straightened out," Lou said. "And bring the girl over to this side of the room and sit her down, too!"

She looked for a relatively clean place to land and sat down holding her raised knees in front of her. She was wearing blue jeans as well. "He happens to be a cop, too, whether you know it or not. Just like you!" she said

"Detective Allen, why don't you show us what's in the bag first!" Lou said.

Ken went to a knee and reached into the open bag to produce a semi-automatic, removed the clip and slid the carriage to ensure the chamber was empty before tucking it in his waistband. No one made any comment!

Next came the riding crop. Still no one said anything.

There was a stun gun, a can of pepper spray, a package of condoms, a dildo shaped vibrator, a jar of Vaseline, all of them laid out on the ground.

Finally Allen produced a wire garrote and held it up like the piece de resistance."

"I suppose you are going to try to make the case that I was going to strangle her," Kroll said with a disgusted shake of his head. "It's for oxygen deprivation at the moment of orgasm or haven't you ever heard of it? It is something Monica and I discussed at length and she was willing to give it a try. Tell him, sweetheart!"

Monica's face was crimson but she sheepishly nodded her head.

Doran, for his part, seemed to be taking the little set-backs in stride. "Is that it?" Lou asked. "No ski mask?"

Ken, like the rest of us, looked puzzled, at first, but quickly recovered. "No ski mask!" he said.

"The girl in Los Angeles said he was wearing a ski mask!"

"What girl in Los Angeles?" Kroll asked. "What is with you guys anyway? What are you trying to pull?"

"The girl gave a very good description of you physically, John, except for your face, of course," Doran said softly. "But an even better description of your car with the stolen California tag. There just aren't that many gold Mercedes GL450's around are there? What is that anyway, a $60,000 dollar car?"

"For what it's worth I haven't been in Los Angeles for three years and I didn't have the Mercedes back then. I had a ....! Never mind what I had! Why should I tell you?"

"You are telling me that you weren't in Los Angeles on the weekend of October 17 this year?"

"No where near it!"

"But you were on vacation from the department!"

"Yes I was on vacation but no where near Los Angeles!"

"Can you prove it?"

For just a second it looked like Kroll was going to tell us but then thought better about it.

"Isn't it up to you to prove that I was there? Why should I tell you where I was on October 17 when I am not sure what this is all about? Am I supposed to have committed some kind of robbery or rape?"

"So you aren't willing to tell us where you were on October 17, but you want us to believe you weren't in Los Angeles." Doran persisted, choosing to let Kroll's curiosity go unrequited.

"This is a bunch of bullshit, if you want to know the truth. And I tell you what. You go ahead and do your thing, whatever it is, and we'll just see what my lawyer has to say about it!"

Very smoothly Lou moved toward the corner where the girl sat cradling her knees and looking a little more worried than embarrassed at this point.

"What's your name, sweetheart?" he asked.

"Monica Worthington!" she answered in a surprisingly tiny voice.

"And how long have you known John?" he asked.

"I know this sounds terrible in a way, but I just met him this morning at the Golden Nugget!"

"Did he tell you where he was cop?" Lou asked her.

"In Arizona," she said. "Flagstaff!"

"Did he offer to take you to Reno for a few days?"

'No!" she said. "He told me he had to be back to work on Monday! We just came up here to . . . ah . . . have some fun and to play the slots. I like to play the slots and he told me that you got better odds in the smaller casinos! We have reservations for tonight at the Stagecoach!"

The sun was starting to slip behind the mountains in the distance and it was getting darker by the minute.

165

"He talked you into driving three hours into the desert to get better odds on the slots?"

Monica shrugged and her face became obviously flushed with embarrassment.

"Glen," Lou said. "Call 911 and get directions to the local police station! We have to get out of here before it gets completely dark."

"Okay, Pal," Ken said to Kroll! "Stand up and turn around. You know the drill!"

Kroll looked at him with a combination of incredulity and disgust. "Are you telling me that I am under arrest?"

"I'll tell you once more!" Ken answered. "I want you to stand up and turn around!"

Slowly Kroll got to his feet and turned around extending his hands behind him. "I am entitled to know what the charge is.

Allen cuffed him and secured the double locks before answering. "You are under arrest for the murder of Caroline Albright!" he said.

"You have to be kidding!" Kroll said. "Who the hell is Caroline Albright? Is she the girl from California? I don't know any Caroline Albright!"

"She's the pretty little girl you hacked to pieces in the Ocala National Forest!"

The words hit him like a sledge. He couldn't keep the surprise from his face. But it was there for only a moment.

"You have to be out of your mind!" he said, quickly recovering. "This is ridiculous! This has got to be the biggest joke of all time! And when was I supposed to be in the Ocala National Forest! "

I was watching the Worthington girl as Ken spoke the words and she had gone suddenly pale. Now she had something else to think about. It was dawning on her that she was possibly destined to become a pile of bleached bones somewhere out in the remote reaches of Death Valley.

With a slight tug of his head Lou signaled to me to follow him outside.

"Here's the deal," he said to me quietly. "If you arrest him on your case the rules are that he be taken up the road to the county jail in Tenopah to await extradition! Which could be a little inconvenient. If I take him on federal charges we can whisk him off to Clark County. When the smoke clears and we analyze exactly where we are on this, and, if the inter-state evidence proves thin, we can always remand him back to Fort Lauderdale!

CHAPTER TWENTY-FIVE

As it turned out the Central Division headquarters of the Nye County Sheriff's Office was a scant two miles away and they sent a car manned by a white haired old warhorse named Ed Smith. Smith listened patiently and without any discernible expression, to Doran's explanation of the circumstances that brought a covey of cops to make what was likely the first arrest in Rhyolite since 1917. Without a word he opened the rear door to his patrol car and stood to one side. We shoveled John Kroll into the back behind the cage where, like any other demented animal, he looked right at home.

We put the girl into the back seat of the Chevy while Bridges took the wheel and I took the other seat. I also had Daniels's cell phone with me. It was a short trip up the highway to C Street the headquarters and en route I put in a call to Roy Peterson in Kingman. We needed a couple of deputies on the mother's house in Golden Valley to ensure that she did not remove any pertinent evidence while they took a search warrant to the on duty judge for signature. It was now 8:30 and there was still enough time to possibly execute the warrant tonight.

"The first thing Kroll is going to do when he gets his phone call is call mommy," I told him. "We need to make sure that the house is sealed!"

The search warrants on the motor home and the motel room, that we expected to be fruitless anyway, could wait. Lou, meanwhile, drove the Mercedes to the Nye County compound to be secured. The plan would be to fly in a team of forensic specialists from the Bureau to process the car.

At the station we moved Kroll into a holding cell where he began to scream about his telephone call and I handed him Glen's cell phone and a couple of us stood by while he called his mother.

"They are going to fly me into Las Vegas tonight and I will be arraigned in the morning!" he told her. "I need to have a lawyer there to represent me. I promise you mother that they do not have enough evidence to hold me but I need a good lawyer to say so!"

"Tomorrow is Sunday," I told him. "You will be arraigned on Monday!"

"Monday, mother! Make it Monday!"

Doran and Allen decided to debrief the Worthington girl in another room and left it to me to knock out a probable cause affidavit with a federal point of view. I found a computer, came up with an outline of the Nye County form and went to work.

Bridges and Daniels grabbed some coffee and took seats on either side of the desk next to me while I hacked away. Just as I was printing out the final copy a huge guy, in civvies, came into the squad room with a badge and semi on his belt. He was every bit as tall and massive as Allen, maybe even a bit larger. He had a completely shaved head, thick mustache and well-muscled demeanor!

"So what do we have here, anyway?" he asked in a casual tone, sweeping the room with experienced eyes.

I scooped the three-page affidavit out of the tray and handed it to him to read, which he did without expression. "Are you the 'Feebee'?" he asked.

"No," I said. "He's in the other room with the girl."

169

He handed the document back to me and opted to go around the corner to take a look at the prisoner.

"Are you in charge here?" I heard Kroll ask him.

"Lieutenant Frank Jansen," the big guy told him. "I'm the Division commander here."

"Well, maybe you could straighten this mess out!" I heard Kroll say. "There is something terribly wrong here. They are trying to frame me for something I never did. They are trying to say that I killed some girl in Florida. First it was Los Angeles then it was Ocala, Florida! The whole thing is very weird! There is something very wrong about this whole thing!"

"I just looked at the affidavit, John, and you know what I think?" Jansen said. "You better get yourself not just a lawyer, but a damned good one! Or you better be blessed with an asbestos fanny!"

When Jansen returned I had moved to the copier with Deputy Smith.

"You know what we have here," Jansen said quietly so as not to be heard from the holding cell. "This is one of those tweener situations that leave you with some difficult decision making. As I see it you have every justification for making the arrest, even a necessity, because there is no doubt in my mind that the girl was consigned to Death Valley. But, unless you have more than you are telling us in the affidavit you are going to need some more weight to carry this thing off in court. You are going to need something tangible that ties this guy to your murder. Do you know what I am saying? More than just the car! And even the car is disputable!"

"Tell me about it!" I said. "When the girl told us that she was all bound up voluntarily our whole plan came apart like my first marriage! We have been following this guy for

170

two months waiting for the right moment to bag him and we managed to pick the wrong one!"

"Unless you were willing to wait until he handed you a corpse. At least you had the integrity to tell it like it was. A lot of cops I know would have leaned on the broad to change her story! Or is that what we are doing now? If you could get her to tell you that somewhere along the line she could sense that the plans had changed you might have a hell of a case!"

"We are planning to execute a search warrant on his mother's house tonight," I said. "We can hope that we will come up with something there. That is our best hope at the moment!"

"Well," Jansen said. "I wouldn't expect too much to come of that. After all, he has a law enforcement background! I wouldn't think he'd be dumb enough to have evidence lying around!"

Doran and Allen joined us explaining that they had turned the interview over to one of the female deputies to make Monica feel more comfortable in a uniquely embarrassing situation.

"Did you find out anything at all?" I asked.

"She is a student at UNLV like we figured." Lou said. "She comes from Cedar City, Utah. A Jack Mormon she called herself. When I asked her why she wasn't home for Christmas she said she was going there on Wednesday. She said that three days at home in a family of nine kids was more than enough. She went with Kroll because she wanted to get away and have a little fun. And he seemed like a fun guy!"

"Does she even suspect that we probably saved her life?" Jason asked.

171

"I think she does. Or at least it's beginning to sink in! Maybe by the time Linda finishes with her the realization will materialize."

Daniels's phone jangled and he was informed that the helicopter was on the ground and refueling at the airport south of town.

We moved Kroll out to the patrol car and the Lieutenant joined Smith in the front seat. The Worthington girl was put in the car with Daniels and Bridges. And Lou, Ken and I hung back to talk to the female deputy without the Worthington girl around.

Linda Montgomery turned out to be younger than I expected, in her very early twenties with a thick mass of blonde hair that spilled down to her shoulders and ran in all directions. She was attractive and wholly wholesome although she had also been on the job long enough to put ordinary embarrassment behind her.

"Monica's just turned eighteen last August, did you know that?" she said. "Just a kid. But she is hip enough to call herself a submissive. In other words she's hot to be mastered and forced to do the kinky things she wants to do in the first place! She wants to be told that she is a naughty girl and be spanked for it!"

"Take the sin out of sex and there goes half the fun!" Allen said.

"So beneath the shy surface our Monica is a smoldering sexpot!" Lou said.

"Exactly!" Linda said. "Kroll must have sensed this and knew how to seduce her. I'm afraid that if asked on a witness stand she would have to admit that everything that happened in the ghost town was consensual. She was pretty shy about saying it, but the guy promised her a once in a lifetime

172

sexual experience, the memory of which she could cling to for the rest of her life! Pretty hot, huh?"

"The guy surprises me really!" Lou said. "The fact that he has a technique or even bothers with one makes him different from most of the serial killers I have seen!"

Linda took a second to drink her coffee before continuing. "He told her that he wanted her to tell him about any kinks or desires she had and to set the parameters of what she would like to experience in precise detail. He said he would not exceed those limits even though, once the game started, she would be required to do everything he ordered her to do without question."

"Just his saying that probably got her panties wet," Ken said.

"And it was working out just great until you guys had to bust in and spoil it. And, by the way, save hr life."

"What about this . . . oxygen deprivation?" Ken asked. "Did she agree to that?"

"He talked her into it, although she had only a vague familiarity with the custom." she said. "I'm afraid that she's not going to help your case at all even though she is beginning to believe that her life was really threatened! In telling the truth she would have to admit that she agreed to everything that took place right up to your intervention! The irony is that, if everything had gone as planned she would have thought that her getting strangled was part of the game right up to the very second she croaked. Her last seconds of life would have ended with the ultimate orgasm. But what a way to go!"

CHAPTER TWENTY-SIX

The Metro helicopter climbed quickly into the black above the desert and leveled out for the run to Las Vegas. Inside we had John Kroll seated in the back row by himself with his ankle shackled to a pin in the floor. His hands were free. I sat alone opposite of him,

In keeping with our plan to keep the two of them separated, the girl was seated behind me facing forward, and opposite Allen and Doran. It was Lou's idea that, because I had the friendliest face in the group, that I should be alone with Kroll in the hope that he might decide to open up. We still needed to prove that Kroll was in Fort Lauderdale on the days in question.

We were airborne for at least ten minutes before either of us spoke, with John appraising me every bit of the way. He wasn't looking so much for a friendly face as much as he was looking for one he thought he could manipulate and I had the feeling that he felt he was looking at one. He hadn't seen the affidavit, yet, and he had to be curious about just how much of a case we had. One could almost see the wheels in his head churning as he tried to figure out what mistakes had led us to him.

"Out of curiosity," he said, breaking the silence. "How long have you guys been following me?"

"Since you came back from vacation," I said. "In October!"

"So you bugged the car!" he said.

"Yes!"

"Did you bug the motel room, too?"

"Not the room!" I said.

"Why not?" He wanted to know.

"Well we figured that you were in this all by yourself, so unless you talked in your sleep there wasn't much point in it!"

"In this? I still have no idea why you have singled me out as what.........some serial killer or something?"

"You're going to find out soon enough!" I said. "Your lawyer will study the affidavit and the reports and fill you in!"

"Are you with the F.B.I.?" he asked.

"Fort Lauderdale!" I said. "The Broward Sheriff's Office!"

"That's a long way from Ocala. Do you have another case you are trying to pin on me besides the one in Ocala?"

He was very good. He was doing a very good job of playing innocent.

"The Ocala case originated in Broward County!" I said, playing along.

"So where am I going to be tried, assuming it gets that far. In Fort Lauderdale?"

"We haven't figured that out yet!" I said and let it go at that.

Kroll snorted again and did his best to appear the incredulous victim.

Silence again. At least another five minutes of it.

"So the Los Angeles thing was a hoax," Kroll finally said. "You wanted me to tell you I was in Fort Lauderdale in October. That was the idea, wasn't it?"

"That was the idea!" I said. "And it obviously didn't work!"

There was another indignant snort. "Well I wasn't in Fort Lauderdale either, for your information. Nowhere near it. A thousand miles from it!"

"Well, at least that narrows it down!" I said.

Behind me the others were making it a point not to listen, involved as they were in continuing conversations. But between Kroll and I more silence. Again, I left it up to him to lead.

"Between you and me I would rather talk to you than those other two. You're more like a human being! You're more like what I think a police officer ought to be! I have the feeling that you, at least, half believe that I might be innocent!"

I decided to let that one go on down the road!

"I suppose that sooner or later I am going to have to tell you where I went on vacation," he said, thoughtfully. "After all it is my alibi!"

"It is going to come up," I said. "And an innocent man ought to want us to know!"

I looked at my watch. It was ten. We would be arriving

at Nellis Air Force Base in another fifteen minutes.

"I was in Mexico," Kroll said.

"Mexico!" I said.

"You probably know that I am an outdoors guy. I go on camping trips almost every vacation. When I was in college on spring breaks I would go camping in some wilderness rather than follow the mob to the Fort Lauderdale strip or the Islands or Cancun! Solitude with nature is more my style. One year I walked the trail through the Continental Divide. On a Spring Break! Not too many people can say that!"

"So you went camping in Mexico?" I asked.

"On a motorcycle with back pack and sleeping bag! But I never did sleep in the open as it turned out! I kind of worried about my personal safety!"

"So you stayed in motels?"

"Yes. But don't ask me the names because I paid no attention to them. They were all pretty much flea bags with Mexican names."

"Did you use a credit card?"

"I had a credit card with me in case of an emergency but I was worried about using it down there!"

"So you paid in cash!"

"Yes!"

"You felt safer carrying around enough cash to do this?"

"I have a secret compartment built into the bike big

enough to carry cash and a gun. I had it specially built. It is a steel sleeve that encloses the gas tank. It looks like the original!"

"Did you take a gun across the border?"

"Yes. A five shot Colt! Once I got through Customs I carried it on me."

"And you were alone on this trip?"

"I started out alone but it seems to be the way of bikers you always pick up company as you go! And it's safer that way, too."

"Whom did you join up with?" I got out my notebook for the first time, deciding to go along with the ruse. He had been read his rights and there was a real chance that he could make an error that could cost him!

"On the way down there were two bikers who were right behind me as I crossed the border."

"Did they have names?" I asked, pen poised.

"Turk and Big Bill!" he said.

"No last names?"

"It's the way bikers are! We pay attention to the first names but forget about the last! They may have given me last names when we first introduced ourselves, but who remembers?"

"So what did Bill and Turk look like?" I asked.

"Bill was kind of bland. Kind of heavy! About six foot three! With balding brown hair! And Turk was a short kind of bowlegged guy with a funny eye that looked like it may have been blind. Maybe cut by a knife! It was a washed out blue with a heavy lid. He had unkempt brown hair like he hadn't washed it for a month and he probably hadn't! He once said that washing your hair too often leads to baldness!"

He went on to create his alibi while I did my best to act like I was taking the story seriously.

Nogales would have been the closest border town going south through Arizona, but he chose to cross over from Douglas because he wanted to see Sonesta and Chihuahua Counties for a reason. His great grandfather on his mother's side had fought with Pershing out of Fort Bliss in Texas and had joined in the yearlong hunt for Pancho Villa back in 1916. He had kept a diary, in vivid detail that was probably worth more than a little bit of money today. He recounted Villa's atrocities as they discovered them. Anyway, he wanted to retrace some of the steps of his great grandfather.

Kroll went on to weave a tale that was too real to come off the top of his head. He was no doubt recounting incidents from a prior experience and bringing it up to date. According to Kroll he had driven to Douglas with the motorcycle in tow and spent the first night at the Motel Six. He found a parking place for his car on the campus of Cochise College where he was confident it wouldn't draw attention at night and took off on his motorcycle.

He crossed the border on Saturday, whatever day of the month that was he said, and joined up with Bill and Turk the first day. The three of them spent most of Saturday at a brothel in Agua Prieta sitting at the out-door bar, but Turk was the only one to partake of the principal offerings by taking one of the girls to a room at mid-afternoon. When they got finally underway later they only got as far as Bavispe the first night. It took another two days to get to Chihuahua.

They spent most of Monday and all of Tuesday in Chihuahua visiting a number of historical sites before going further south into the midlands of Mexico.

They took their time along the way, with little side trips to some of the picturesque little towns that were pretty much the same as they were a hundred years before. There were tiny adobes along dirt roads with chickens running around loose. There were small chapels with Franciscan monks in their brown cassocks.

It was like going back in time! Kroll claimed that it was a lot of the same Mexico his great grandfather must have seen.

Kroll stayed with his buddies until Friday when he had to turn around. They had gotten almost as far as Durango when they parted company. On Sunday afternoon he stopped for lunch in another little town, the name of which escaped him, and ran into another American headed north. His name was Greg. He was a muscular body builder type, who worked in the oil fields around Texas City. And they stuck together until they reached Douglas.

"Did Turk and Bill tell you what they did for a living?" I asked.

"They had worked at a Saturn plant in Kentucky if I remember right. And they both got laid off in the cutbacks. So they decided to bike it to Mexico City."

"Did you tell them that you were a cop?" I asked.

"It came up about the second day! And, by the way, if you look back over your shoulder you can see the lights of La Vegas starting to come up on the horizon! It's quite a sight to see the city spring up out of the darkness!"

We had been traveling in pitch black above the desert

and there in the distance a low level of flickering lights danced like the dying embers. I got up, removed the cartridges from my revolver and re-holstered it before sitting alongside Kroll one seat removed. It was fascinating to watch the long stream of lights rise out of the ink.

"Did you go to college, Detective?" Kroll suddenly asked.

"Yes!" I answered.

"Four years?" he asked.

"Yes!" I said.

"Well, I am willing to bet that in those four years there were at least two, not just one, girls missing, murdered or raped while you were there."

"None that I recall!" I said.

"Then it had to be a small college or you just weren't paying attention!" he said. "And, for what it is worth, in October, on whatever the date in question, you were in Fort Lauderdale! Are you beginning to get my point?"

"I get your point!" I said.

The neon extravagance up ahead of us had risen to full bloom by now and we were sidling northward and well above it, crossing the boulevard and abreast of the blue and white lighted runways of Nellis Air Force Base. Before we had any sense that we were ready to land we were on the ground.

CHAPTER TWENTY-SEVEN

The helicopter came down on the landing pad at precisely 10:20 pm. Two uniformed officers were standing nearby with both a marked and an unmarked vehicle. Kroll was handcuffed again with his hands behind him and led to the patrol car where he was whisked off to the county jail. The other car was left to the four of us. Allen took the wheel and I got in the back seat with the girl.

As we drove to the city our silence was interrupted by the jangle of Lou's phone.

"Uh-huh!" we heard him say several times. His expression did not change. I had a hunch he was talking to Martin or Peterson about the search warrant and I would have felt a lot better if I was able to see something more reassuring in his face.

"The truth is, there is no such thing as a predictable pattern!" Doran said, at one point. "Was the diary on the shelf or lying in the open?" we heard him inquire. More listening followed.

"Ok, Lieutenant," Lou finally said. "Thanks for the report!"

This was not good. If the search warrant had turned up something I was certain he would have said so even with the girl in the car. It was beginning to look like we had struck out in Kingman, too.

"Anything good to report?" Allen asked.

"Not really!" Lou said and let it go at that.

We had turned on to the quiet end of Las Vegas Boulevard and were rolling toward downtown when Monica, oblivious to the significance of the phone call asked me for my name.

"Jim Kilbane," I told her.

"Are you from Las Vegas?" she asked.

"Florida!" I said. "Fort Lauderdale!"

"Well, Mr. Kilbane," she said, "or I guess it's Detective Kilbane! I've been thinking it through. And I know how it all looked when you found us. But I still can't believe that John has done any of the things you suspect. He's far too nice and far too balanced. I know you must have your reasons to believe otherwise but you will have to go a long way to convince me!"

Allen took his eyes off the road long enough to study her in the rear view mirror but neither of us decided to reply. We were within a few blocks of her apartment so why go into it. When we arrived Ken helped carry her suitcase to the front stoop and Lou waited until he returned before telling us what we were waiting to hear.

'Not a thing, guys! We completely struck out!" he said. "Martin said that when they got to the house they were informed that the mother didn't even have a key to John's room. 'He was a neat freak!' she said. 'And he didn't want anything in the room disturbed!' They had to pick the lock to get in.

"And everything turned out to be consistent with what a neat freak's room should look like. Everything was arranged just so! Everything neatly folded and all in a line! But, very unfortunately, there was nothing of value to the case to be found. A complete zero."

"Are you surprised by that?" Ken asked.

"Frankly, I am." Lou said. "Especially with the mother locked out of the room!"

"Was there a safe in the house?" I asked.

"There was a safe in the closet of the mother's bedroom and she cooperated by revealing its contents. The jewelry was pretty obviously hers, although they photographed all of it.

Then Lou turned around to face me. "What did Kroll come up with for an alibi?"

I related the story of the trip to Mexico and Lou listened patiently until I was through.

"They found the great grandfather's diary," Lou said. "There was a worn leather-bound relic of a diary with a tarnished gold clasp. It was inconspicuously enclosed in a line of books on a single shelf. The searcher opened every book on the shelf and a picture dropped out of the diary. And you won't believe what it was?"

"At this point is there anything that could surprise us?" Ken asked.

"It was a picture of Kroll and a short guy with bow legs in front of a monument with an eagle on the top and some kind of government building in the background. And on the back it said, 'Turk and John . . . Angel of Liberty . . . Chihuahua, Mexico . . . October 13 . . . THIS YEAR!"

"He set it up for an alibi!" I said.

"Why would he do that when he did not have the slightest reason to believe that he was apt to be a suspect? Did he mention to you that there was a picture to back up his story?"

"No!" I said. "But he did mention the diary! He mentioned his great grandfather's service to explain why he wanted to go to Chihuahua and that was natural enough. But he didn't mention the picture because it would have made it look a little forced."

"Are you trying to tell us that you believe that he really did take the trip to Mexico in October?" Ken asked Lou.

"Could he be that subtle? That smart? Could anyone?" Lou asked. "To prepare an alibi when he didn't have the slightest reason to believe he would need one and to plant a picture and not bring it up as proof when the matter was being discussed?"

I thought about the care he had used in separating his car from Caroline's at the Lauderdale Beach Hotel. He had arrived hours after her and left before her. "I think he's that smart!" I said. "I think if we didn't find the picture he would have had an eureka moment later on. He would have suddenly, by the way, remembered that he even had a picture that would prove he was in Mexico in mid-October!"

Lou, turned in the font seat, stared at me for a full minute at least.

"Jim, have you ever had a case when all evidence pointed to an obvious suspect whom you have arrested or were about to arrest when out of the blue some redeeming evidence comes into the picture?"

"Once!" I said.

"A case where your original suspicions seemed so supported that you found it almost impossible to let go?"

"Once!" I repeated.

"What we need here is a fresh approach. We need a devil's advocate. We need to bring another detective into this picture to take a look from the other side. I'm thinking about this guy Forrest who was at our meeting in Flagstaff. He seemed to me to have the right balance of thoroughness and skepticism. And he has a familiarity with the case. I would like to fly him in here to take a statement from Kroll on Monday."

"I can handle that," Ken said. "I will get in touch with him!"

"I will handle the arraignment on Monday and we have enough to hold Kroll for at least twenty-eight days while we scramble around to fill in the blanks. You, Jim, are going to have to go back to Fort Lauderdale to start seeing the people and asking the questions that we have been avoiding in order not to run the risk of Kroll finding out we were looking at him. We've got Ken here in Las Vegas and Roy in Kingman and between the three of you turning over the rocks we have left sitting we should be able to conclusively determine if Kroll really is a killer or not!"

CHAPTER TWENTY-EIGHT

It had been a long day and the adrenalin boost made it difficult to sleep. I laid awake thinking about the complexities and disappointments of the case and eventually got around to remembering Kevin McCloskey. Doran had asked if we ever had a case where everything pointed to an obvious suspect who turned out not to be a suspect at all. For me that was Kevin McCloskey.

One of my earliest cases when I was doing white-collar crime years ago involved a couple that took over the management of a twenty-four unit motel in Lauderdale By The Sea called "The Spyglass"! The owner, a guy named Bremer, had to return temporarily to Hoboken, New Jersey, to run his father's furniture store while the latter recovered from a serious operation. He needed someone to manage his motel while he was gone. The McCloskys answered the ad, and the fact that she had she previously operated a motel in Belize tipped the scales in their favor.

The early bank statements sent north showed a slight decline in occupancy during the peak season and Bremer suspected that his managers might be making a little extra money on the side with the proceeds from a few of the rooms but let it ride. But in January there were zero deposits followed by calls from one of his maids that his managers had apparently taken off. His loss of revenue amounted to approximately $50,000 dollars.

The application files included a driver's license of each of the suspects as well as the address of her mother with whom they lived for a few months when they came back from Belize. A check of the records showed that Kevin was arrested in 1994 for disorderly intoxication and I found that Debbie Gibson, using her maiden name, had been arrested for possession of marijuana in 1990. Turning their mug shots into photo lineups Bremer and his maids were able to pick them out without any difficulty.

But when I visited the girl's mother in North Lauderdale things were different. Surprisingly, she said that, although there was a marked similarity between her son-in-law and the person in the picture, there was something different about him that was difficult to explain. She also said that she had no use for Kevin, and that she sensed from the first time she laid eyes on him that he was no good. Yet she insisted that the guy in the photo lineup was not her son-in-law, while, at the same time admitting that the girl was her daughter.

To me, and it seemed everyone else, the driver's license picture and the mug shot of McClosky were one and the same. She even agreed with the consensus description of a guy who was 6'1" tall with balding red hair and a thin mustache!

Suspecting that she had some motive I couldn't understand I filed for warrants anyway.

The Assistant State Attorney in Case Filing was an attractive, sophisticated, ivy league type named Bobbie Simonds who, after making her marginal notes on a copy of the report looked up at me while tapping her pretty nose with her pen.

"I'm bothered by the fact that the mother-in-law says he's not the guy in the lineup!"

"I know," I said. I can't figure why she would want to mislead us!"

"He lived with her for a few months so she knew him

best and was able to discern some subtle difference! I think we have to give that a lot of weight!"

"Could she have possibly had a relationship with him?" I asked.

"Does she look like a hottie?" Bobbie asked.

"She's not bad," I said. "Hotter than her daughter, actually, who is somewhat of a frump!"

"Well, under the circumstances, I think we should file on the daughter and leave him open for now. If you get her you will have him if they are still together. And if they have split up by then she will certainly be willing to help you find him!"

About a year later Sergeant John Caruso approached my desk waving a report.

"Does the name Kevin McClosky ring a bell?" he asked. "Well, he's just filed a report that someone used his identity to obtain a credit card and proceeded to max it out in motels and retail stores from Florida to Georgia."

That night John and I visited Mcclosky's apartment and he was more than happy to invite us in.

"Where is your wife?" I asked him.

"My wife?" he asked with a quizzical look on his face. "I haven't seen her in ten years and as far as I know she still lives in Plantation. Why do you ask about her?"

"I'm talking about Debbie," I said. "Weren't you legally married?"

"Who's Debbie?" he asked. "I don't know any Debbie!"

I was unconvinced while giving him high marks in playing the part. He let us check the closets for women's clothing before I asked him, "Did you manage the Spyglass Motel for three months last year with Debbie Gibson?"

He really looked puzzled and I could sense that Caruso was buying his performance. "I never managed a motel in my life. I am a carpenter by trade and I just got back from Belize!"

There it was! Belize again!

We showed him the photo lineup and he just laughed. "The guy looks something like me alright, but it's not me!"

"Do you mind if I bring a witness over to check you out! Will you be going out tonight?" I asked.

"You want someone to identify me?" He asked.

"If it's okay with you!"

"Sure, if it is going help you clear up some misunderstanding. Apparently we have a guy who is using my identity who looks like me! He must have seen me in person somewhere to get the idea to pull this off!"

"Well we do know he was in Belize at one time!" I said. "It could have been there!"

By this time Bremer had sold the motel and moved north and my best available witness was Mrs. Gibson, so, while Caruso babysat the suspect I drove over to North Lauderdale to collect the mother-in-law. On the return trip across the county I suggested to her that I was more than a little concerned that Debbie was no longer with McClosky and, if Mrs. Gibson was telling the truth, not in touch with her either. It could mean that something serious had happened to Debbie!

While we remained in the car with the headlights on, Caruso marched the suspect out to stand in front of the beams.

Mrs. Gibson didn't take long. "He's not my son-in-law!" she said emphatically. "He looks enough like him to be his brother but it's definitely not him!"

"What differences do you find in the two of them?" I asked.

"Mostly it's around the eyes. My Kevin looks . . . well to put it bluntly . . . he looks sneaky. I guess it's the best way to put it. Sort of deceitful! Devious! And, oh, by the way, he had a kidney removed when he was younger. He said it was from a football injury. He has a major scar on his lower back!"

I asked the sergeant to have McClosky turn around and raise his shirt and his back turned out to be as smooth as a baby's behind!

The trip back to North Lauderdale was mostly achieved in an uncomfortable silence. I had no doubt that the matter of the kidney scar was contrived to throw us off the track. What I couldn't figure out was why she would cover for McClosky and not try to come up with some alibi for her daughter! I even found myself glancing at her from time to time while I pondered the possibility that she was sexually involved with her son-in-law. For a middle-aged woman she was no slouch.

Sergeant John Caruso, meanwhile, took the scar business to heart. A tall, good-looking highly intelligent guy, he was somewhat of a legend in the business of fraud investigation. He had already retired after twenty-five years with Fort Lauderdale and was readily welcomed by the Sheriff's Office to an extended career. He was so uniquely trusted that judges would routinely sign his warrants without even bothering to read the narrations. The joke was that his glove compartment was stuffed with pre-signed warrants so that all he had to do was fill in the date and the details!

By the time I got back to the station to put our thoughts together he was standing by the fax machine waiting for a picture. I was there with him when it landed in the tray. It was an arrest picture of a guy who was the image of the McClosky we just left, complete with balding red hair and mustache. Only the name was Sean Smith! He was just two years older than McClosky and he had one prior conviction for identity theft.

"It was the way the old lady described the kidney scar," John said simply. "It sounded like a butchered job. I had a hunch it might have been removed while he was in prison!"

CHAPTER TWENTY-NINE

The telephone rang at 7:00 am and my awakening was the only affirmation that I had ever slept at all. I had lain awake for hours recalling the McClosky case and it was like a book you couldn't put down. Around 3:30 in the morning I finally invaded the liquor cabinet to down a couple of small bottles of bourbon that may have helped a little.

The plan for the day was to meet Flanagan for breakfast and then Doran was going to drive us to Fredonia to get our things from the Coral Cliffs while Lou checked us out of the hotel. Then Flanagan could wait for Daniels for a ride to Flagstaff while I returned to Las Vegas with Doran. I needed to make a reservation for a late night flight home.

In the shower I started thinking about the McCloskey case again.

Sean Smith and Debbie Gibson were arrested in Oklahoma City within hours of a presentation on "America's Most Wanted" and by then were using even another identity of Leo and Debbie Kowalski. I recalled John Walsh, in his recap the following week commenting, "This type of criminal is able to shed one skin and take on another the way you and I change socks. Molting season for them was any given month of the year!"

Thinking about that statement hit me right between the eyes! As soon as I dried off I checked my notebook and flipped back to the weekend before Thanksgiving and Kroll's trip to East Santa Fe Avenue. And there it was! Among the row of western stores was the Pony Express Postal!

It occurred to me that John Kroll was one of two things. He was either innocent as hell or smart enough to cover all of his bases. He would have to be smart enough to create alibis before they were needed! And likely smart enough to already have an alternate identity to cover his tracks.

I could see him with another driver's license, credit card or cards, along with a separate bank account. He could have used the other cards to pay for motels and gas along the way to Fort Lauderdale. It was more probable that the alter ego would be that of someone dead or entirely fabricated. He could have gone to the private mail drop that Sunday to pick up the credit card bills from his vacation.

From my time in white collar I knew that private postals could appear to be residences or places of business and the box number appear to be an apartment or an office suite. It was done all the time by scammers and identity thieves.

I was going to have to change my plans and go on to Flagstaff with the other cops.

When Flanagan joined me for breakfast he wanted to hear all about Kroll's arrest and the setbacks that followed. Then I braced him with my thoughts about the Pony Express Postal.

"I could handle that for you," Richard said. "There really isn't any need for you to go out of your way!"

"We'll handle it together!" I said. "I'm not under the gun to get home exactly! Another day won't make that much difference!"

Doran met us in the lobby and we loaded our luggage into the trunk of his Trans-Am. You could count on Lou, no matter what doubts may have crept into his mind about the case, to be the same unflappable self. And I really got the sense that he had obtained some considerable doubt about whether or not John Kroll was truly guilty.

He let me take the wheel and as we negotiated the winding exit out to Sahara Road he began to expound on his love for Las Vegas. "I mention all of this," he said, "because if it turns out that we don't have enough to prosecute John Kroll, after all this investment of time and money, my next assignment is likely to be International Falls, Minnesota!"

"International Falls is really nice in the winter," Rich said, from the back seat. "I've been there! You're going to have to get a quality set of sunglasses to keep from going snow blind!"

"Not to mention an electric blanket for my car!" Lou added.

"Do I detect some gathering doubt about John Kroll?" I asked.

"It's a question of how smart is this guy?" Lou said. "I've been an agent for twenty-five years and I have never run into anyone quite this bright if that's what it's all about!"

"More like shrewd!" I said. "He has an animal-like cunning! And I've seen more than a few just like him!" And I went on to tell him about the Pony Express Postal theory.

Lou listened with growing interest and appreciation. "You know something?" he said. "You may really have something there. He may even have a safety deposit box somewhere where he keeps his mementos, too. Or maybe a metal box in the woods! It's hard for me to buy into the idea that, assuming he is a psycho, he hasn't stored something somewhere. It's supposed to be a part of the serial killer M.O."

"And the Mexico thing," Flanagan said. "You know

they scan your driver's license into a computer now as you cross the border. On the 14th he probably went in to Mexico as Kroll and came out the same day as the alias. And later did the opposite. So if you checked on Kroll alone the crossings would have supported his alibi."

We were leaving Las Vegas by now and headed into the barren hills on the way to Utah. We found ourselves quietly admiring the multi-colored desolation around us.

As if reading our thoughts Flanagan noted, "When you consider that this is what the mob saw when Bugsy came up with the idea of using mob money to build a lavish casino in the middle of nowhere no wonder they shot his ass!"

My phone began to jangle and I slid it out of the holster and handed it to Doran.

After listening for a few minutes we heard Lou say, "You've got to be kidding! Really! What a break just when we needed it! We just passed the Nellis exit but we can turn around and go back. I would say we could be there about three hours." He glanced at his watch. "We could be there about 2:00 pm. Listen, thanks, Lieutenant, for thinking of us. I really appreciate it!"

Doran closed the phone and handed it to me. "Turn around at the next exit and head back. We are on our way to Kingman!"

"What happened?" Rich and I chorused.

"You aren't going to believe this. But the lady who lives within sight of the Kroll residence saw the commotion last night and thought that there must have been a burglary. After mass this morning she approached Mrs. Kroll to inquire. When she was told that it was a search warrant the neighbor had the good sense to keep her lip buttoned. Her son is a carpenter who installed a hidden safe in John's bedroom several years ago. It was a graduation gift for the kid who specifically requested it. Naturally Mrs. Kroll never mentioned it to the cops last night. Naturally she is going to claim it skipped her mind!"

"What kind of kid wants a hidden safe for a graduation present?" I asked.

"I would say one who has some special things to hide!" Lou said. "And so the cops are going to go back on the original warrant! And Lieutenant Martin was thoughtful enough to think we might want to be in on it! However, there is just one little thing to worry about! "

"What's that?" Richard asked.

"If the old lady called John this morning to tell him about the search last night he could have told her to clean out the hidden safe. She would have had a few hours to do it before the county got a couple of deputies with their eyes on the house. It would be a question of whether or not John believed that we were eventually going to find out about the hidden safe!"

"And they are going to wait for us?"

"Well they need to go back to the judge to get a Sunday exception added to the warrant. And they are bringing the carpenter up from Las Vegas to show them how to get access! But if Kroll had a chance to think it through he well might figure that at some point the hidden safe could surface. He might well have had his mother empty the contents this morning!"

"Or," said Richard, "he might figure with what they didn't get last night he is home free!"

CHAPTER THIRTY

We were a small convoy turning off of Highway 68 and on to Verde Road at 4:00 in the afternoon. Including the carpenter, Marty Lucas, there were four cars and a police van. We traveled along the paved road through a half-mile of wilderness before seeing a solitary house and another quarter mile before there were three. All of them were large and spacious but the house of Edna Kroll was the most intriguing. It was a split-level adobe behind a chain link fence. Of the three, hers seemed to blend best with the ruggedness of its surroundings. Inside the fence, on a gravel driveway was more evidence of prosperity and that she was home, a late model Cadillac. We all lined up in a row on the gravel swale and emerged like a mini-invasion, nine of us in all.

Mrs. Kroll seemed very reluctant to answer the door and we had to lean on the bell a couple of times before it opened as far as the chain would allow.

"I think I better talk to my attorney," she told Lieutenant Martin in a small voice after he advised her that we were doing a follow-up execution of the warrant. "I believe that twice in two days could well be considered harassment!"

'Mrs. Kroll, the warrant is good for seven days and we went back to the judge to get permission to serve it on Sunday! You could have saved us a lot of trouble if you had told us about John's hidden safe yesterday!'

She looked over Martin's shoulder to see Lucas right behind him and shook her head sadly. "Marty, you had no right to tell them about the safe," she said, with the typical illogic of the ill fated. "It's absolutely none of their business!"

"This is a legal process, Mrs. Kroll," Martin said. "And you are going to have to open the door or we have every right to kick it in!"

Reluctantly she complied and stepped back out of the way as we trooped in. As Lucas went by she added "You shouldn't be involving yourself in this, Marty! You have no obligation to help the police!"

"Mrs. Kroll," Marty answered. "They are looking for a hidden safe! I'm sure you wouldn't want them tearing your walls apart, now would you?"

Even on a Sunday afternoon alone she looked primly professional. She was wearing the blouse and skirt she had probably worn to church that morning and saw no reason to change. Her white hair was neatly bobbed and, with her rimless glasses, she looked like she had just finished teaching Sunday school and possibly had.

"We expect to find some incriminating evidence which you are free to witness on John's behalf if you like!" the Lieutenant offered.

"No thank you," Mrs. Kroll answered, holding up her cell phone. "But I am going to call my attorney!"

Flanagan opted to keep her company in the living room while the rest of us filed into the bedroom and Lou and I took positions against the far wall to stay out of the way. Martin and his team began to remove the hanging clothes in the closet and pile them on the bed. I could see the back wall of the closet had an unusually ornate design that featured a pattern of protruding but well spaced wooden nipples. Lucas stepped forward and began to unscrew four of them in the lower right corner of the wall.

Lucas was a wiry, athletic fifty, with an energetic manner who had offered to cut off his weekend in Las Vegas without the slightest hesitation. He was more than a master of his trade in that he had a small company that did every manner of custom carpentry.

"There are only six of these that will turn," he said. "And they are Japanese screws that open clockwise! I needed to see the wall to remember how I did it. I've done over a hundred of these jobs in the last ten years and everyone is a little different!"

Once the screws were removed the panel tilted enough to lift away from the baseboard. Inside was a safe with a combination lock. A feeling of excitement began to register in all of us, especially Lou and I who were hoping to be pulled back from the brink of what seemed, less than two hours before, a failed, very costly investigation!

"I don't suppose there is any point in asking mother if she knows the combination," Martin said, as he scoured the sides of the safe and the immediate surroundings. "Almost everyone records the combination on something nearby rather than trust their memory!"

I found myself looking at the books that lined the shelf in a single line. The leather-bound diary was there. Interestingly, there were several books on psychology, O'Hara's book on Criminal Investigation, one on IQ, and a red cloth bound dictionary. I pulled down the dictionary.

The fly leafs were empty except for where Kroll's name was meticulously scrawled in a manner that indicated a training in calligraphy. I flipped the pages open to the word "safe" and it was clear. Flipping further to "vault", however, was different. There was the tell tale sequence of numbers written neatly across the top of the page.

"Are you ready?" I said calmly. "I believe I have the combination!" Everyone looked at me in amazement but I had run into it once or twice before!

"Starting at zero! Twelve left. Three right!" And on through the combination until there was an audible click.

Martin had the video guy set up his camera on a stationary stand while trained on the safe. He took a deep breath and said, "Here goes nothing!"

The door swung open and we were staring at an array of what appeared to be, at first glance, incriminating evidence. There were two shelves above the bottom of the vault. The shelves we piled with plastic baggies containing anything from jewelry to hair and even teeth. A yellow manila envelope rested on the bottom on top of more plastic bags and three boxes of what appeared to be bank checks. At the very bottom, underneath it all, was one of those green, cloth covered auditor type journals.

"Here we go!" Martin said to the camera and lifted the first bag to identify it. "It is a closed plastic bag that contains a yellow metal ring with a red stone surrounded by smaller white stones!"

Lou looked at me with something akin to a smile of relief. It had to be Robin Woods' missing ring! We had all we could do to keep from cheering out loud. One by one the plastic bags were lifted, identified and dropped into a large plastic garbage bag and duly noted on a property receipt form by Roy. There was no neat pattern about the bags.

Most of the baggies contained what appeared to be pubic hair of varying quantities, or near lack thereof, given contemporary tonsorial customs. One of the bags was crammed with shimmering blonde hair that could have been Caroline's.

When the bags were all compiled they numbered thirty-five and led us to believe that there were more victims than we had estimated. The manila envelope was next. It contained a driver's license, two credit cards and a bankbook all in the name of a Gerard L. Shepherd with an address of 136 East Santa Fe Avenue in Flagstaff. On the license was a picture of Kroll with the familiar crooked smile.

The checkbooks also bore the Shepherd imprint and the Pony Express Postal address!

"There is probably some duplication here," Lou said, with a shake of his head. "Between the jewelry and teeth! But how many bags of hair do we have?"

Roy ran down the list before answering "Twenty-three!"

"No wonder he visited his mother so often," Flaherty said. "He must have come up here to the privacy of his room to get his jollies fondling the bags and reminiscing! That's what these guys are supposed to do!"

Last came the journal that Martin opened and perused carefully, looking around the room before returning his attention to the camera.

"The journal appears to be a handwritten account of some of his experiences!" he said. "There is a prologue! It begins with the words, 'The first living thing I ever killed was a beautiful Palomino horse with large luminous eyes! And the fear the eyes registered at the moment I buried the axe between them gave me a thrill I will never forget!"

Martin had to stop! "This is going to be brutal!" he said, flipping through more pages before reading another couple of lines. "Chapter four!" he announced, his eyes running up and down the page. "Standing before me stark naked, with her wrists handcuffed behind her, she seemed to sense what was going to happen to her! She began to pee. I felt the urge to slide beneath her to accept it but I couldn't risk the vulnerability! We were miles from civilization in the middle of the desert and so I ripped the tape from her mouth so I could have the pleasure of hearing her scream!'' Martin had to stop and catch his breath.

"The asshole could write!" Flaherty blurted and immediately regretted the insensitivity.

"Having worked in New York I didn't think there was much more that could shake me up," Martin said as he leafed through a flurry of pages. "Chapter Nine! Listen to this! 'They were so young their tender little pussies had no signs of hair! I decided that having two of them doubled the pleasure in what was to come!..........''

"Okay, Lieutenant, we are getting the idea," Lou interrupted. "Give it a quick run through and see if he mentions any names!"

The lieutenant scanned through several pages before answering, "He does not seem to. I guess he is keeping them anonymous like the baggies! On the other hand he does mention some locations! He mentioned the beach in Del Ray!"

"How many chapters are there?" Lou asked.

Martin went to the end and said, "The last chapter is numbered twenty-two!"

"Twenty-two!" Lou exclaimed. "And one chapter has two girls! And we have twenty-three baggies with hair. It looks like a perfect match! And when we get the DNA matches Kroll will be buried in circumstantial evidence!"

My own thoughts were on Caroline and on how horrifying her last moments had to be. I was tempted to ask Martin to read the last chapter but I wasn't ready to hear it at the moment. Sooner or later I would have to include it in the case, if it seemed like a probable match, not that we wouldn't all be better off not knowing.

In order to safeguard and minimize the handling of the collected evidence it would be stored at the Mohave County Sheriff's Office to be made available for trial. The plan was for a representative of the FBI to remove partial hair samples from each of the baggies to submit to the lab in Washington for DNA testing, a procedure that would be taking place over the next few months.

CHAPTER THIRTY-ONE

At 8:30 am on Monday morning Deputy Richard Flaherty and I were the first to arrive outside Room 103 of the Federal Building in downtown Las Vegas, where John Kroll was to be arraigned. In short order the others arrived from home.

At fifteen minutes before the hour an overly nourished bailiff came, with noticeable effort, slogging down the long corridor to stand with his knees braced inward like a sleeping horse, while he sorted through his keys. With a brief nod to the four of us he unlocked the door and, without a word, stepped aside to allow us to precede him. The four of us took seats in the front row to the immediate rear of where the attorneys were to be seated at their tables.

The expectation was that the plea would take only a few minutes and then Doran, Flaherty and I would head out to Fredonia to complete what we started out to do the day before. The last of the Flagstaff Chevrolets would be waiting for Flaherty at the Coral Cliffs and after we gathered our belongings and checked out I would return to Las Vegas with Lou to fly out to Fort Lauderdale in the early evening. It was really no surprise to find the four of us sitting in an empty courtroom because word of Kroll's arrest, important as it undoubtedly was, had yet to gain any media attention.

The next to arrive was Miss Kelly Johnson, an assistant to the United States Attorney, an attractive young lady in a neatly tailored business suit that, nonetheless, failed to completely neutralize her sexual assets. Even her work-like medium-heel shoes were of little help in that effort. Added to that, her immaculate nearness on a bleak Monday morning had the effect of a third cup of coffee!

We all stood as Lou introduced us all around before Kelly slipped through the gate to plop her brief case on top of the table. Then she said to Doran, "He's got himself a good attorney, Lou. An expensive one! Edward F. Grace. Do you know him?"

"I've heard of him of course!" Lou said.

"I know him very well," Allen said. "We've locked horns a few times over the years! He's a straight shooter and smart. A former Green Beret who served in the Gulf War!"

"And speak of the devil," she said, looking over our shoulders.

Grace turned out to be a middle-aged guy with matinee idol looks tempered to only a slight degree by a height less than average. His generous mane of brown hair bordered on disheveled and his shoulders were as wide as he was tall. Like most successful criminal defense attorneys there was a marked likeability about him.

He dropped his bag on the other table and came over to introduce himself. "Guys, I don't want to upset you at all," he said, 'but I have gone over the reports, talked with our girl, Monica, and have been informed about the lack of results of the search warrant and I find the entire case a little thin. Just so you know, since this is Christmas week, I am going to ask for the bond hearing this morning and I am going to try to get John released on is own recognizance. He has no priors and is a police officer, after all, and I do not see him as any risk to take flight. Not with what we have for a case so far! To tell you the truth I wish we were going to trial tomorrow!"

Kelly's mouth fell open realizing that Grace apparently didn't know about the second search. The mother must have not bothered to inform the attorney about the discoveries from the hidden safe. Martin had provided Mrs. Kroll with a copy of the evidence, dropping it in her lap, while she sat numbly. Apparently she had not yet been able to deal with the bad news.

"There is something you need to know, Ed," she said quietly. And proceeded to fill him in on the previous days events.

Grace bent over to listen with a nodding head and by the time she was through he was standing up straight. "I take it that we are going to play with the same rules," he said dryly, "that no matter how the verdict comes down I get to go home!"

"I believe you may be more inclined to enter a plea of not guilty by reason of insanity!" Kelly said.

"You may have a valid point, there," Grace said, with a straight face. "I may have to begin coaching him on how to carry on an intelligent conversation with one of his shoes!"

"Kroll," Allen interjected, "is very apt to claim that he bought the entire collection from some guy named Jose when he was in Chihuahua!"

Grace laughed out loud. "Stop giving me ideas!" he said.

A door at the other end of the courtroom sprung open and three guards came in surrounding two prisoners handcuffed together and dressed in orange flannels. One of them was Kroll. Somehow he still managed to maintain his air of disdain. Grace made his way over to prisoner's bench to advise Kroll that there had been a change in plans but the nearness of the other prisoner negated any opportunity to discuss details.

A male and female had entered the room and took seats several rows behind us and I had the feeling that they might be press. Another lawyer made his way down the aisle to take a seat next to Grace's.

Then our pudgy deputy was back to make the age-old salutation. "All rise! Hear ye! Hear ye! Hear Ye! The United States Federal Court is now in session. The Honorable Judge Christopher Roberts presiding!"

The judge, tall and regal, swept in through the door, with his robes bristling and climbed the platform to advise us to all be seated.

The prisoners had their hands freed so they could stand separately, but their feet were still chained together.

"Ralph Neyland please stand!" The judge ordered. "You have been charged with the robbery of the Nevada Mercantile Bank on December 18th and are suspected of several other robberies as well. As to the robbery of the 18[th,] how do you plead?"

"Guilty, your honor!"

"So noted. And we will advise you and your attorney of a date for sentencing. Until then you are to be held without bond!"

"John G. Kroll, please stand!"

Kroll shuffled to his feet.

"You are charged with the pre-meditated murder of Caroline Albright in Fort Lauderdale on October 17th and are suspected in numerous other incidents regarding missing young girls. As to the murder of Caroline Albright, how do you plead?"

"Not guilty, your honor!" Kroll said without hesitation.

"So noted! You are to be held without bond for trial and possible rendition to Broward County, Florida to be tried by the State of Florida! Is that understood?"

"Yes, your honor," Kroll replied.

"Does anyone have any other business before the court?"

No one did. And the judge's robe-swirling exit was even quicker than his entrance

Grace had gone over to confer with his client while the guards re-handcuffed him to his companion. And Kelly turned her attention to us. "It looks like you have everything you need for a prosecutable case, but my advice to you is to go back home and dig up everything you possibly can. Be ready to pour it on! Leave no stone unturned! Don't just try to win the game, make sure you run up the score!"

"You're right!" I said. "There is more of the case out there to be had. I'm sure of that!"

Grace had returned to the table and singled me out. "He wants to talk to you alone!" he said.

"He wants to talk to me?" I answered. "Without his attorney present? That's a little unusual at this point, isn't it?"

"I advised against it but he continues to insist. And, unfortunately, he has the right to overrule me! My feeling is that there may be something he wants to tell you that that he thinks might buy him some leniency! Maybe he is going to tell you he had an associate or something. Who knows?"

"Maybe the barber," Flaherty said.

"It wouldn't be the barber or they wouldn't have had an entourage when they went bike riding on Saturdays!" I said. "But there could have been a connection in Fort Lauderdale. He may have been staying with some friend, which would explain why he went there in the first place! But when does he want to do this? I am scheduled to fly at midnight tonight."

"He wants to see you right now!" Grace said. "As soon as they get him back to the county jail!"

I looked at Doran.

"We can wait for you," Lou said. "We're not pressed for time! It's probably just that he wants to bounce a few things off a friendly ear. But it's still worth a shot!"

CHAPTER THIRTY-TWO

The Clark County Jail had a conference area in which prisoners normally meet with lawyers, but no one felt that comfortable in allowing John Gerard Kroll access to such a populated place. Therefore I was forced to meet with him in his cell, where he greeted me, hand extended, more like an ally than antagonist.

During my career in law enforcement I tried not to play games with bad guys in custody who made a pretense of having information you can use in order to spend a lot of their time wasting yours. Unless there was some real reason to believe that they would be genuinely forthcoming there wasn't a lot of point to it. Most of the time they were leading you down the primrose path much preferring to spend their time in some conference room with you as opposed to sitting in a cell! And the con, for them, was an enjoyable pastime.

And slapping the mugs around in the hope of getting information was strictly amateur night. It didn't work at all, unless you just wanted to force them to say what you wanted to hear. It wasn't a really effective method of obtaining new or unbiased information. So at the very outset of this meeting with Kroll I was already planning my exit.

"Fort Lauderdale!" Kroll finally said. "It's got to be great being a cop in Fort Lauderdale. Somehow I think that if I had been a cop in Fort Lauderdale I wouldn't be in the trouble I'm in now!"

"Just how do you figure that?" I asked.

"I don't know!" he said. "It's just a hunch! Based on

211

my relationship with you, I've got the feeling that cops in Fort Lauderdale are more apt to stick up for each other than they are around here!"

"That's a nice little fantasy," I said. "And you be sure to hang on to it!"

"The main reason I wanted to talk to you is that I could easily see that you were head and shoulders smarter than the rest of those cops and a lot more experienced! I know that you have your job to do," he said, "but I could sense that, privately, you have a hunch that I might have been framed!"

"I'm sure your lawyer told you that we found your hidden safe!" I answered.

"My mother told me last night!" he said.

"And you didn't tell your lawyer about that this morning?"

"I didn't have time. Anyway, she told me that they found plastic bags with hair and jewelry, none of which I know the first thing about! Someone must have planted that stuff!"

"Someone would have to have know about the hidden safe to have done that," I said. "To say nothing of having to break into your mother's house!"

"There were others who knew about the safe," he said. "I had three high school friends who knew about it. We used to hide our porn there. Plus my writings which were very controversial!"

"I thought the safe was a graduation present," I said.

"It was during the summer before we all went away to college! And you know how that goes. Three guys have probably told how many others we can only guess!"

"It's almost like there was no point in having the safe hidden to begin with!" I said.

"Exactly!" he said. "But you know how kids are. I couldn't resist telling a few of my friends! It was a point of excitement to me! Something mysterious! I can see now that it was a big mistake to tell anyone about it at all!"

"So you called me over here to tell me that you were set up?" I asked.

"I am telling you that if you get me out of here I will find your killer for you in a matter of weeks. Maybe days. I happen to be a very good investigator if you don't know that already! I am a very good cop! But sitting here in jail I can't be any help to you at all!"

"Not that I am going to knock myself out following up on it, but maybe you could give me the names of the others who knew about the safe!"

"Well, that's the point! They certainly aren't going to admit it to you and become a potential suspect! But they can't deny it to me! I showed them how it worked!"

"So the baggies were planted," I said. "How about the driver's license with your picture on it in the name of Gerard Shepherd!"

"That's another important clue!" he said. "Whoever is behind this had to have some connection to the Motor Vehicles Division in order to pull it off. Unless the license was a forgery!"

"Which brings us to the journal! Detailed accounts of numerous murders of young girls! In your handwriting!"

"Now that's the central point! Those are my writings! All fiction! I've been writing those stories for years. Only a few of my closest friends knew about it! I would take an incident like the disappearance of Angela Sacramonte and use my imagination to put myself in the position of the killer. I would make it all up but the reader would be able to experience exactly what the real killer must have felt! I made it as kinky and exciting as I could in order to give my readers the actual effect of being there and doing those things! And don't tell me that people don't want to vicariously explore the forbidden because they do! Look at the violent video games they turn out these days. But this is what made me vulnerable to being set up. They've got games where they shoot cops and run over pedestrians with cars! I am just trying to take them to the next level of exciting, but forbidden experiences. The writings could be construed as actual accounts. This is precisely why they chose me to set up and divert attention from themselves as suspects!"

"And the fact that the twenty-two chapters include twenty-three girls and the number of baggies with hair happens to be twenty-three was just a coincidence!"

"Again the point exactly! Whoever did this saw that I had twenty-two chapters! I'll bet you are going to find that some of the hair in those baggies is not from victims at all! Maybe the hair was picked up from a barber shop floor for all we know! If you find that there is duplicate DNA in two or three of those baggies it will be conclusive proof that I was set up!"

"So your stories are based on actual events? Stories you have read about!"

"Most of them are. I selected stories of missing girl because they gave me free reign to elaborate. There was no crime scene to box me in. Some of the stories, though, are entirely made up from scratch. If there were no missing girls to write about for an extended period of time I would make one up out of my imagination! I just got a kick out of it!"

"All things considered I really don't think I am the right guy to help you, John," I said. "I just spent two months trying to nail you for the murder of the Albright girl! You might think about getting your lawyer to hire a private eye!"

"Well you have to feel some regret that a truly decent, honest guy like me is behind bars! A fellow cop! Totally railroaded!"

"For some odd reason regret is not what I am feeling at the moment," I said.

"Well, the whole thing is ridiculous. What possible good is going to come from locking me up?"

A little bell was tinkling in the back of my brain. I thought I was beginning to get the picture.

"Let me ask you something, John!" I said.

"Go ahead!"

"Speaking just hypothetically. Let's just say for the heck of it that you really did kill all these girls. Are you trying to tell me that it would be a waste of talent and potential to lock you up and throw the key away?"

"Are you trying to trick me with that question?" he asked suspiciously.

"No, I am just trying to see where you are coming from. We are just speaking hypothetically!"

He stared at me for a few seconds before answering. "Well let me ask you a question. Still speaking hypothetically. Let's say, for the sake of argument, that I did kill those girls, which I didn't! Would locking me up change anything? Would it bring the girls back to life? You have to weigh all the good someone like me could do for the world in the overall consideration! And that's what makes the difference!"

"Well let me ask you something else!" I said, because the daffiness was beginning to intrigue me. "On another subject altogether! You used to be a cop........."

"I am a cop!" John interrupted.

"Okay, you are a cop! And let's say you bust a guy for armed robbery! Put him away! Should the same rule apply? If the culprit has some redeeming qualities, should he be spared his prison time?"

"I can see your point," he said.

"Well what about it?

"There could be some mitigating factors in deciding his fate!" he said. "But it is unlikely! In my mind anyone who steals money from decent, hard-working people ranks just above child pornographers as the lowest of the low!"

I went out of there with my head swimming. I thought I had gotten used to the zany logic of the sociopaths who comprise the majority of repeat offenders but this guy took it to another level. To the sociopath one plus one equals two when it suits him, or her, but, otherwise, any answer will do! Kroll was perfectly willing to recognize that, while the killing of 23 girls might have been unfortunate, and for some an inconvenience, the practical thing to do was to let bygones be bygones and move on from there!

CHAPTER THIRTY-THREE

The red-eye out of Las Vegas was surprisingly packed and, if the mood of the passengers was markedly more subdued than it was when we were headed in the other direction, there didn't seem to be many complaints. The dollars left behind could be chalked up to the cost of entertainment and there was no denying that they had been suitably entertained. In one sense, though, I turned out to be the biggest winner of them all. And that's exactly the way I felt!

In spite of the adrenalin rush, immediately upon take-off I was lost to the world! And that, too, was no small wonder. Monday had been an exhausting final day.

Monday had begun with the arraignment, followed by my jail interview, and after that a hastily arranged national press conference conducted in the auditorium of the MGM Grand! Sheriff Rooney had flown in from Flagstaff and he and Lou Doran gave a rundown of the arrest while glossing over the details of the evidence located in the safe. No mention was made of the journals because of their sensitive nature and because none of us had read them through as yet.

There were pictures of Kroll, of Caroline Albright, her car, his car and several of the missing victims that comprised such a sad gallery of pretty faces. Doran made mention that the suspect had been kept under surveillance for over two months by a task force that included officers of several agencies, and he listed the agencies without mentioning our names. He also said that there were still some loose ends that we are tying together and, officially, the case was still under investigation.

There followed the usual queries from the media who, as usual, in order to be seen and heard, found a dozen different ways to ask the same few questions before Doran was finally able to drop the curtain.

John Gerard Kroll had now become headline news!

Immediately after the press conference Flaherty, Doran and I took off for Fredonia to finish our business there. Lou had received the financial reports on Gerard Shepherd and ran through them on the way. As expected Shepherd's credit card had been used at various points along the trip to and from Florida in October. One surprise, though, was the fact that on the nights of the 15th and 16th it was not used for lodging, indicating that he must have been staying with an associate in the Lauderdale area.

"We need to find the person he stayed with," Lou instructed, "and you ought to make that the first order of business when you get back home! What we don't need is for some friend of Kroll's to come forward with a phony alibi!"

When we reached the Coral Cliffs there was still some beer in the refrigerator and so we all sat around in the living room to take on the torturous task of wading through the copies of the Kroll chronicles. They had to be read. We needed to affirm that they were, in fact, accurate accounts of the killings.

We could hope he made mention of the fact that he hacked the girl to death in the Ocala National Forest, which he would have no way of knowing if, indeed, he had been in Mexico at the time.

It was a tough go! If you were to draw up a list of perversions it was likely that Kroll had covered them all. In fact it seemed to be his basic intent. He engaged in only one incident of cannibalism but it wasn't to be omitted! It involved the two young girls from Del Ray who he described as ideally tender for the purpose. "Exquisite!" he exulted, at the end of the chapter. "Delectable! My compliments to the chef!"

Necrophilia occurred on two occasions, and one of them involved digging up a body that had already been buried in a shallow grave!

He most often omitted the kidnap phase of the incidents and more often than not the disposition of the bodies, preferring to concentrate on the sexual content! And the killings were all by strangulation. In the case of what would appear to be Robin Woods he went from beginning to end. A harlot, he called her, who more than willingly got into his car and was taken out into the desert near Ottoman where he raped her anally, a technique that had not become, as yet, part of her arsenal.

"But he made her enjoy it!" he claimed. "And enjoy it enormously making it almost a waste to deprive her of the thrill of ever doing it again!"

He took her body to the muddy banks of the Sacramento Wash and stuffed her into the mud, expecting her to sink from sight. But her head remained disconcertingly above ground her brown eyes staring at him as though asking him why! "Why? Why? Why? I gave you what you wanted! Then why?" he wrote as a conclusion.

It got worse than that at times as we plowed through the material, me, with one eye on the clock. My flight was scheduled for midnight but we wanted to squeeze in dinner before our three-hour drive.

While he mentioned puncturing the "tennis player's" tires in Chapter Sixteen there was no mention of it in Chapter

Twenty-Two.

His last chapter spoke of a girl so beautiful that she could have lived if she could have just shown him an ounce of appreciation prior to discovering his sexual skills! "I took her to a farm near Pahokee," he said, omitting entirely any mention of how he came to possess her, "where the fall harvest had just concluded! And to a migrant farmers' hut where the mattresses still remained on the beds."

He went on to say that he gave her a shot of heroin to "heighten her compliance" and worried that the dosage might be too strong for her in her uninitiated state! As, in all of the accounts, he prided himself on his sexual skills if not his prowess and his ability, as he saw it, to arouse passion at every turn.

"When I was fully inserted she lay passive and non-responsive," he wrote of our presumed Caroline.

"She was determined not to be an ally to any of it. And I laughed in knowing that her passion would soon overwhelm her sense of propriety. As I applied the garrote and began to squeeze it around her neck she began to struggle. Her pelvis was an integral part of that struggle and it was the involuntary movement of her lower regions that brought her to the early stages of excitement.

"When I released the pressure she relaxed for only a second. She looked at me with eyes that were now hooded. Smokey! Sultry! And it was she who commenced the pelvic grind to which I, with equal eagerness, responded. Once again I cut off her air and she thrashed around wildly. I was tempted to once again relieve the pressure. To allow her to live! But instead I continued on to dispatch her to her Maker in the throes of ecstasy!"

He went on to say that he spent the night at a motel

with the girl's body inside the car under a blanket. And the following morning drove north to the forest where he, having bought a hatchet and a rain suit in Ocala, hacked her beautiful body to pieces.

The earlier rundown of the credit card charges of Gerard Shepherd revealed that he had stayed at a motel in Okeechobee on the night of October 17th.

I was the first one finished. Not once had I applied a single note to the legal pad beside me. It did not seem to be necessary. It was all subject to anyone's interpretation except for the hacking of Caroline's body in the Ocala National Forest. That particular account, as far as I could see, had sealed Kroll's doom.

The only other problem was how to get the chronicles in front of a jury and out of the public eye, perhaps a slim possibility. For one thing the claims if not the revelations would tear at the hearts of the loved ones and shock the sensitivities of the rest of us. It could be enough to turn Stoddard Lee into a Jack Ruby. They would have to bring John Kroll into court clad in medieval armor. The John Kroll accounts were, easily, too rough for public consumption.

Our plane had arrived at the gate and we were soon moving down the aisle, through the telescopic tube and out to where the friends and relatives of the disembarked waited with the usual anticipation. The tanned, rested face of Captain Murray Abrams stood out, grinning from ear to ear. He was one of those who got fresher as the day wore on and meeting me in the ungodly hours of early morning was no effort for him. If the others around us had risen in the middle of the night it was probable that my Captain had yet to go to bed.

"Congratulations, Lieutenant," he said. "I knew you could do it! What little you lack in luck you more than make up for in effort. Either way you have fulfilled my best expectations and gotten the Sheriff off the hot seat!"

"Well, we still have a couple of loose ends to deal with," I said. "We think Kroll has a friend somewhere in town, maybe an ally. And we want to make sure that no one comes up with a phony alibi for him."

"And you have no comment at all concerning your promotion?"

"Are you kidding me? I thought it was a slip of the lip!"

"No slip of the lip and it came straight from the Sheriff himself. Effective at midnight you are officially promoted!"

CHAPTER THIRTY-FOUR

To say that Doctor Kevin James was British was to belabor the obvious. His 250 pounds spread evenly over a five by five frame and his booming, mellifluous baritone gave him an extraordinary impression of power! In his thirty odd years in this country he not only retained every ounce of his accent, but flaunted it! With an obvious disdain for habitual barbering he had even managed to turn an expanding forehead into a dominant impression of hair.

James had agreed to meet with me at his office on a near empty campus on the Sunday between the holidays and was now comfortably settled behind a ponderous desk while busily engaged in the ceremonial rite of igniting his pipe.

"I've been following the recent events closely," he proclaimed at his stage left best, "and I must admit to being totally caught off guard! Not that I ever thought John Kroll was not without missing pieces. But for him to be identified as a murderer is beyond belief!"

"That seems to be the consensus," I said. "Everyone seems to think he was somewhat eccentric but there didn't seem to be any suspicion that he was psychotic! What was he like in class?"

"He was bright! But not brilliant! A fairly good writer, although with a bizarre imagination and he was the most unpopular student in class!"

"Why was that?" I asked.

"He was arrogant to a fault. He was always pitted

223

against the class in one argument or another! He was convinced that he was the only real talent in the class which, to some extent, may have been true! And he had an odd way of assimilating information that, somehow, got twisted in the processing. He would interpret the writings of others differently than the rest of us and then get into major arguments with the class about it. He saw hidden meanings and symbolism where none were intended. It was an odd quirk to an extent I had never encountered before or since!"

With a look of satisfaction he finally got his pipe perking. "He had a girl friend, you know!"

"I didn't know. Who was she?"

"Her name was Calley Carson and she was as popular as he was not. She was a farm girl from Pahokie without a solitary pretension. She had a sense of humor that she brought to good stead in her relationship with Kroll who seemed to have none at all! No real wit, anyway! She always seemed more bemused by him than attracted. And if genetic indicators are to be taken seriously it was my opinion that she was a latent lesbian, anyway!"

My phone had started to ring and I looked at James for permission to interrupt!

"Go ahead," he said. "I'm in no hurry!"

It was the remarkably calm voice of Louis Doran. "Are you sitting down?" he asked.

"As a matter of fact I am," I said as I watched the professor puff contentedly on his particularly aromatic pipe while studying some corner of the ceiling.

"John Kroll has just escaped!"

It was a jarring piece of news. Flashes of what had to be

an unappreciated genius crossed my mind. The guy was a top security project. Even his rendition, scheduled for the 17th had been planned with extreme caution, three agents to accompany him on a chartered plane! Yet with all this he had managed to escape!

"When?" I asked. "How?" Doctor James, sensing my reaction, had returned his attention to me!

"About forty minutes ago!" Lou said/

"How?"

"Well, that's the thing," Lou said. "We don't think it was his plan but someone else's and he just happened to luck out. So Far!"

He went on to relate how three prisoners were brought to a dentist on Sunday when the office would have normally been closed. The dentist was the only one in the building other than the group from the jail. When, after treatment, they emerged from the elevator into the open, parking area beneath the building, shots were fired and a car sped away. When the dentist went down to the parking lot to investigate he found two dead guards lying in pools of blood. The prisoners were gone!

"One of the prisoners had a broken tooth that we think was done on purpose," Lou said. "That's why we think the escape plan was his!"

"So the car took them all away?"

"We're not sure! If Kroll and the other guy were left behind and running the streets in orange jailhouse grubs they aren't going to get far. The whole area is crawling with cops!"

"And if the mugs took them with them they are just as

apt to blow them away!" I said. They are, after all, witnesses to the shooting of two cops!"

James was really listening now, although he had no reason to believe that our conversation was concerned with Kroll and there was no particular reason to tell him.

"As it happens," Lou said, "I have the weekend detail so I will be on top of what happens and I will keep you posted!"

"Trouble?" James asked when my focus returned to him.

"A little!" I said. "About the girl! It's really imperative that I talk to her. She might be his only friend in the world!"

"Not likely! Not at this point, anyway! They had a major falling out before he transferred out of here."

"Do you know of any way that I can get in touch with her?"

"Well, she graduated three years ago. And I would not be surprised if she was doing post-graduate studies somewhere. But the Carson farm is somewhere in Palm Beach County. That would be the place to start!"

In the walk to my car the phone rang again and it was Lou once more. "Well they picked up one of the guys. A guy named Wells. And we have a clearer picture of how it went down."

He went on to tell me that as soon as the group arrived downstairs there were three guys in ski masks waiting for them and they opened up without the slightest hesitation. When the cops went down they freed Walker, tossed the keys to Wells and ran for the car. Wells freed himself first, then tossed the keys to Kroll! Wells took off running. Thirty minutes later someone spotted Wells trying to open a locked dumpster and used his cell phone to alert the police!

"So Kroll is still on the loose in the orange grubs!

"So far!" Lou said. "I'll keep you posted!"

CHAPTER THIRTY-FIVE

On Monday bodies began to surface. At mid-day a motel manager in St.George, Utah decided to enter a room that had shown no signs of life for a particular reason. The lifeless form of James Walker was discovered slumped on the floor between twin beds with a single gunshot wound to the right temple and the semi-automatic next to his right hand. Not only was there no suicide note, but whoever orchestrated the event apparently was unaware that the subject just happened to be left-handed.

Our theory was that Walker had been sprung from the jail with some kind of reciprocal arrangement in mind, an arrangement that had obviously fallen short of someone's expectations.

Not much later the body of a middle-aged male was found in a utility closet in the Corte Building about a block from the medical building where the break took place the day before. He was clad in his undershorts with orange jail garb nearby along with the bloodied hammer that had smashed his skull. John Kroll was still at large and manifestly desperate to remain so.

Meanwhile I had located Calley Carson through her utility billing, in a cozy, tree enshrouded adobe on Center Street just one block from the ocean. I had done a complete pedigree of her social and financial information before I made any attempt to interview her. The background check showed no criminal record, that she was part owner of a lounge in Wilton Manors and had neither received nor sent any long distance calls in the past twenty-four hours.

There is no best time to visit the owner of a bar but I took a first shot at just before ten o'clock Tuesday night. Her roommate answered the door clad in a mini-robe and slippers. There was no way to mistake her for the description I had of Calley. This girl was a black haired Barbie, tall and slender and as I was to learn later, a recently divorced convert with a nine-year-old son.

It was one of Calley's nights to close the business that, again, I was to learn later, was a saloon that catered primarily, though not entirely, to young ladies with no noticeable interest in men. While the struggles of a pained economy threatened the survival of too many small businesses "Calley's Place", thanks to its theme, was thriving!

I had to come back later or wait until what would have to be, for a bar employer, a sluggish morning.

So over an hour past midnight I sat waiting in her driveway until her small pick-up truck took the turn on a minimum of wheels. I was getting out of my car when she jumped out of hers not the least bit cautious about some guy in the dark.

"Are you a cop?" she asked, immediately, no doubt prompted by the recent news concerning her former boyfriend. Calley was wearing jeans, a red plaid shirt and a she had a baseball cap perched on the back of her head with the peak at a rakish angle. She looked like a post adolescent boy.

"Come on in, Lieutenant," she said after she reviewed my identification. "We've all been reading about John, so I've been more or less expecting you!"

I was sorry to see her attractive companion had gone to bed but, on the other hand, there was enough personality in front of me at the moment to account for the three of us. Calley was, as Professor James had suggested, without pretensions and eminently likeable. In the first thirty seconds I was completely apprised of her current living arrangements while she went to the refrigerator to get us each a beer.

She moved a living room chair closer to the couch so that our knees were nearly touching, except that one of her legs was under her as she sat down.

"What would you like to know about John?" she asked with a smile that went ear to ear. "My screwball ex-boyfriend! I suppose I ought to be more appalled at the things he apparently has done but that part of it hasn't hit me yet! It's all so hard to believe!"

I filled her in on the news about the escape that, some-how, hadn't been sufficiently publicized as yet!

"He's a guy on the run right now," I said. "He needs an ally badly. He needs someone with him to register at motels, get food, until his face gets off the front pages and the television screens and people will start to forget what he looks like. We're thinking that he might try to contact you!"

She scoffed at that idea. "Not a chance! We really had a blow-up at the end. I even tossed off a few punches that had him staggered I'd like to think! Knowing now what I didn't know then I'm very lucky he didn't kill me!"

"If you'll forgive me for saying so," I said, "it's a little hard to put the two of you together!"

She laughed again. "And I was just as dykey then as I am now! But he seemed to be intrigued by the syndrome!"

"And how about you?"

"I'm not any different than most lesbians, I guess, in

that I can get it on with a guy if I want to. And there are some of us who occasionally get the urge for a little cock. I've got a straight bartender at the club who claims that he's never had it so good! In the few months that John and I were linked we probably had sex four times at the most. And I was seeing a couple of girls on the side. Which, by the way is what our big fight was all about! We're all lucky we didn't get killed!"

"Aside from the sex did you find any comfort in his company. He strikes me as not a lot of laughs to be around!"

"We were busy. Between work and school we were both very busy! I was living at home on the farm. Our time together was limited. Since we were in class together and seen together everyone else saw it as a committed relationship when it was really just a casual friendship! But you are right about John. His range of interests was pretty limited!" Her bright blue eyes took on a sharper hue. "Can we be honest for a minute? Can we cut to the chase? Do you want me to tell you what you are probably dying to know?"

I had only the slightest idea where she might be headed with this. "Why don't you do that?"

"We were both into bondage! That was the big attraction! He liked to tie me up and I liked to have it done to me! It's as simple as that? You get yourself tied up and helpless and a few blows with the riding crop and you are in the home stretch to orgasm city! He understood the psychology and knew how to exploit it! Sex also happened to be his one topic of interest whenever we talked. Kinky sex. But I had no idea that he was all about killing. And why he didn't kill me back then when he had me completely at his mercy is beyond me!"

"It was because you were associated with him publicly!" I said. "Everyone knew you were close! If you had

231

turned up missing he would have been the most immediate suspect! That's the only reason you are alive today!"

"I guess that's it!"

"Let me ask you something else? Do you use migrant workers on your farm?"

"At harvest, yes! What does that have to . . ! Oh, you arc asking if John and I used the shelters? How did you know that?"

"He wrote about it in his journals!"

"About us?"

"No about the Albright girl. The one case where we wound up with a body! We think he used one of your shelters!"

"Really! He wrote about all this. A confession?"

"He's going to claim the journals are fiction. But tell me! How many huts are there on the farm? And did you use any particular one?"

"There are eight! And we tended to use one of the two middle ones. After the harvest we turn off the electricity and take away the blankets, but there are still mattresses on the beds. It is very dark out there so we brought one of those battery powered hurricane lamps with us."

"We are going to have to do a forensics check of the rooms tomorrow!"

"I'll tell my father! Unfortunately it is going to confirm suspicions about me he has had since high school! But why should I care now! Do you want another beer?"

"No thank you!" I said. "But go ahead and get one for yourself. I just have one more thing to talk about!"

She leaped up and strode to the refrigerator and was back in a few seconds, this time propped on top of the other leg! "Fire away!"

"Thinking back to John's time at school was there any other close friend of Kroll's you can remember? Someone he might have stayed with for two days last October when he visited here?"

"Absolutely," Calley answered. "What makes it easy is that John collected friends the way the Chicago Cubs collect pennants! He only had one that I knew of! And if you think John was spooky you should have seen this guy! His name was Donald Riverton, IV, and it makes you shudder to think that there had to be three of them before him."

"I take it from your use of the past tense, you haven't seen this guy lately!"

"Not since school! And he dropped out the same year that John transferred. I don't have a clue what happened to him!"

"How spooky was Donald?"

"He could have made Stephen King shit his pants! Now if it turned out to be Riverton on the news right now none of us would have been surprised. He was a kind of squirrelly looking, thin little guy with a funny sounding, nasal kind of voice. He had stringy long brown hair parted in the middle; the kind of dry looking hair that you knew would soon be saying bye-bye! He and John were big into snuff pornography! Pictures of pregnant women with their bellies split open. That kind of thing! The stuff that comes from Denmark or Africa or someplace!"

"Whose porn was it?"

"Donald's! I would see the two of them poring over the stuff in the study hall. All blood and gore. I used to tell John that he should drop that guy. That he was dangerous! That seems oddly funny in knowing now how things turned out!"

"Did Donald have money? Usually us ordinary folks don't bother to keep track of the lineage numbers!"

He seemed to come from a reasonable amount of money, although he and his mother lived in a modest old house in downtown Fort Lauderdale right on Andrews Avenue. It was one of those small stuccos that sat right up close to the street. Every time I go by the house I think of him but had absolutely no inclination to see if he was still alive or living there!"

"He lived with his mother?"

"His widowed mother! John and I got the use of the house just once when she and Donald went north for Christmas! Like I said it was a very small house! Hardly enough room for us to play naked hide and seek!" she said while laughing uproariously!

CHAPTER THIRTY-SIX

For Donald Riverton, IV, with his apparent anti-social asexuality there was seemingly not much prospect for a fifth. By noon on Wednesday we knew just about everything there was to know about him. The most important thing we found was that he received a phone call on his cell phone from Las Vegas at 4:10 pm the previous afternoon, the length of which seemed to indicate some problems in persuasion!

We also found out that Riverton had been employed for a few years as an x-ray technician at Broward General Hospital but since his mother's death in the latter part of the year had chosen to be unemployed. Therefore there was a better than even chance of finding him at home in the early afternoon.

The small stucco, on North Andrews, had the slatted windows that characterized old Florida and, like its immediate neighbors, sat close enough to the passing traffic to feel the breeze. The driveway, of necessity, ran the length of one side of the building and to slow down enough to make an entrance was to invite a chorus of horns. There was no answer to the doorbell chimes and a cursory walk to the back affirmed that there was no one home at the moment. My phone jangled and it was Doran!

"Have you talked to the Riverton guy yet?" he wanted to know.

"I'm at his house right now but he apparently isn't home!"

"Well get out of there as fast as you can without being

seen. And when you are clear of the place call me back and I'll explain!"

To enter the driveway nose first meant that you had to back out onto the high-speed drag and you needed the intervention of the lights further back to create a break in the flow. I really thought I might not pull it off. It was reasonable to believe that Riverton could be along at any minute.

But I finally made it out and went south a few blocks before taking Third Street west. Finding a metered parking spot I pulled off the street.

"This morning Riverton booked a flight for Flagstaff," Doran said. "For tomorrow! New Year's Eve! I have a call in to Abrams right now! We are going to want you to be on the same plane! We have to believe that he is going to meet up with Kroll and this is our shot to bag him!"

"I'm your guy," I said.

"The flight has changes in St. Louis and Phoenix and we know we are dealing with a master of misdirection. So it is possible that Riverton could separate himself from the plane in either of those two cities. However, the way the security system is supposed to work is, that if he has luggage going forward on a plane that he has not boarded everything is supposed to shut down. The baggage is supposed to be found, searched and removed and a lot of notoriety would attend the whole process. So it is unlikely that Kroll would risk any of that kind of attention.

"However," he continued, "if Riverton gets on board with just carry on, we have to be alert to that possibility!"

"So you want me to eyeball him when he leaves the house tomorrow! To see if he has heavy luggage!"

"That and to see what he looks like and what he is wearing! We are all going to want to know that! We are planning to have two agents meet you in Flagstaff and we will have his car rental bugged."

CHAPTER THIRTY-SEVEN

At 4:00 pm on New Year's Eve we were on the ground in Phoenix waiting for the flight to Flagstaff and Riverton was pacing nervously up and down the concourse that led past the gates. At times he wandered out of my line of sight but, by now, I was convinced that he was going the distance so I sat tight with my eyes shut and my head sagging as though I was grabbing forty winks between planes.

There were not a lot of people waiting, no more than thirty, so that one in particular tended to stand apart and off to one side. He was in his middle thirties, not overly tall, but with a linebacker's build. He had a serious mien about him and his pale blond hair had the look of early thinning but what remained had changed its mind and decided to stay. He was leaning against a dividing wall with a coat slung over his shoulder Sinatra-style.

After a bit he straightened and walked over to me.

"Are you Kilbane?" he wanted to know. "I'm Evans, FBI!" He had a deep resonance with a lot of carry, a fact that worried me more than a little because Riverton was now coming back down the concourse in our direction.

"I take it the guy in the green sweater is our pigeon!" he said, without looking behind him.

As if sensing the oddball's approach without turning he lowered his voice to a near whisper. "The asshole is pretty nervous, isn't he?"

"With good reason," I said as quietly as I could. "I'm a

little nervous myself!"

I wondered what Evans was doing in taking the risk of talking to me. In his business suit all he needed was some sunglasses and an earpiece to complete the picture. A semblance of a smile might have helped soften his federal agent image but it apparently wasn't worth the effort. He finally elected to sit down beside me and I noticed that the preoccupied Riverton did not seem to be aware of us at all as he continued on down the corridor in the opposite direction.

"They didn't tell me that I would be meeting an agent in Phoenix," I said.

"It was a last minute decision," Evans said. "They caught me just as I was leaving the office. Apparently they are expecting a shootout tonight and they wanted to prop up the odds!"

"Is there a reason they picked you?" I asked. "Have you done this kind of thing before?"

"You know I never have!" he said. "How about you?"

"I worked anti-crime for a few years," I said. "This kind of thing got to be routine!"

"Well, from what I hear this guy Kroll has even more experience than you!"

The public address system finally announced our flight and Evans and I got into what was a very short line. Riverton finally came along to take his place at the rear.

"I hope you have a jacket with you," Evans said, "because it's snowing in Flagstaff and about 40 degrees!"

I wasn't sure if Evans and I looked right together with him in a business suit and me in a sweater and jeans but again Riverton seemed so preoccupied that he didn't seem to be looking for signs that he was being followed. With a wide choice of seating Evans still chose to sit next to me. Riverton came down the aisle past us without so much as a glance in our direction.

In the hour to Flagstaff I learned everything I needed to know about Tom Evans and the same went for him. He had fifteen years with the Bureau and had been assigned to posts from Kentucky, Minnesota and now Phoenix. He was married with no kids. Lately he had been working large-scale economic fraud.

About twenty minutes into the flight the pilot announced that, due to the weather, we might be diverted from landing in Flagstaff and that would have thrown our entire game plan into the hat. But a few minutes later he was back on to tell us that we were cleared for landing as planned.

CHAPTER THIRTY-EIGHT

We flew into Flagstaff in a blizzard of snow that had turned the runway into a toboggan run; the last flight in before the airport shut down.

With so few on the plane there was no reason to stall around but by the time Evans got his overcoat out of the overhead compartment, Riverton had already brushed by us, still nervous and preoccupied. He was rail thin and had, somehow, managed to nurture a prison-pallor in the land of perpetual sun.

At baggage claim as soon as my bag came off the turntable I found a place off to the side to unzip it and remove a leather jacket before heading out into the snow. I left my gun where it was for the time being. Heading for the door I could see the now jacketed Riverton heading toward the Hertz booth at the far end of the terminal.

As soon as I caught up with Tom, a taller, well-muscled guy, obviously working off a picture of me, approached us. His name was McLeod, and he was surprisingly young, at most on the underside of thirty. It had always seemed to me that the Bureau must have hidden its young in offices anywhere until they were mature enough to be seen in public. But then it was the FBI who invented Swat about the time they blew up the Symbionese Liberation Army headquarters in Los Angles back in the sixties. My guess was that the obviously able-bodied McLeod was specially assigned to this little excursion with the anticipation of trouble at the other end.

When we reached the Land Rover at one end of the

parking garage across the street my suspicions were confirmed. Upon our arrival another young agent popped the back lid for us. He was already wearing a navy blue flak jacket and inside we could see three more for us, as well as a shotgun cradled on each side of the trunk area.

The other kid's name was Donovan and he was as rangy as his partner was ripped. "You may as well put the flaks on now," he said, as we tossed in our luggage. "And you can get rid of your coats because the jackets can keep you plenty warm!"

We did it quickly knowing that Riverton was due to cross the street at any moment. I unzipped my bag and got out my trusted Smith five shot .38, which didn't seem to instill a lot of appreciation in my partners-to-be. I also took my one speed loader and slipped it into a pants pocket. They, undoubtedly, felt a lot better about the .45 caliber semi-automatic that Evans brought to bear, although there was no comment, either way, as we hustled into the car.

Donovan got behind the wheel and McLeod turned around and handed me a photo stapled to a white piece of paper. It was the usual FBI release on bank robberies. It contained a surveillance shot of a heavily built guy at the teller window, wearing a cowboy hat with raggedy hair falling all the way to his shoulders. On the table in front was a blue steel revolver much like my own. The flier stated that it was the robbery of an Arizona Mercantile Bank in Henderson at 3:00 pm on December 30th. The head was tilted at an angle so that the hat covered part of his face.

"Does that look like your guy?" McLeod asked.

I took a second to study it in the dim light of the garage. "Maybe yes and maybe no," I said. "I wouldn't rule it out!"

"We think it was him!" McLeod said. It was fair to say

that the agent's personality was even more phlegmatic than mine.

"Where did he get the gun?" I asked.

"That's another reason we think it's him!" McLeod answered. "The guy he hammered in the Corte building had a gun like that in his car's glove compartment. It's a Smith just like yours! And we think Kroll is still driving his car."

We could see Riverton finally emerge from the terminal and make his way across the street to the parking garage and to the section allotted for Hertz rentals.

"We have an agent at the rental desk in case he pulled some kind of a switch on us," Donovan said from behind the wheel. "Apparently everything is go!"

CHAPTER THIRTY-NINE

Riverton's rental was beginning to move and we saw the cursor move out on to the street and start south working its way toward #89 north.

"How much did he get in the heist?" I asked.

"Just over three," McLeod said. "And like a real pro he dropped the bills around the dye pack and left the teller window with a real mess!"

"That's pretty sophisticated," I said. "Maybe it wasn't Kroll."

McLeod didn't say anything but handed me back the picture. I studied it more carefully. "It could be him!"

"If it is we know what he's got for a weapon!" McLeod said.

"We think, anyway!" Evans said. "You never know with this guy!"

"We know he's a weapons guy!" Donovan said. "He applied for Swat with the department and kept bugging them about it. And we took the time to make sure we didn't have any pawnshop burglaries in and around Vegas, so we're pretty sure he's got the one gun. A five shot revolver!

"So I take it we are going into this thing with just the four of us," Evans said.

"That depends," said McLeod. "If the situation allows we will call for additional backup. But if we get more than an hour from Page or Flagstaff we are going to be on our own!"

During the steady descent to the desert floor the snow had turned to a cold, driving rain and we continued to maintain a much closer tail than before. We were approximately a mile to the rear. It now seemed that I spent a large part of my recent career being led around by a GPS receiver.

We went on by the Kroll trailer still sitting up by the power plant and it was getting prematurely dark beneath the clouds.

"I half expected the weirdo to want to stop for dinner but it is obvious, in looking at him, that food is not a major consideration!" Donovan said. "I hate going into one of these things on an empty stomach!"

"Jimmy could have a three course meal before his own execution," McLeod said. "As for me I wouldn't be able to eat a thing right now! It's funny how that works!"

"There is a medical study that says that tension will target either your head or your stomach but not both!" Evan said.

"Tension?" Donovan asked. "We're just four guys in flak jackets riding out to meet a guy who has already killed two dozen people! Why the tension?"

We had passed Cameron Station and were now headed west along the highway with the headlights on. It was like my old stamping grounds with the now-familiar landmarks along the way.

"It looks like we are headed for Fredonia," I said.

"It kind of does! And it doesn't surprise me!" McLeod said. "I'll say this! This guy Riverton doesn't spare the horses. He's clipping along at 75."

"Kroll has a buddy in Fredonia who is good with guns," I said.

"We know," McLeod said. "But they haven't been in contact unless it's by carrier pigeon! Besides Kroll knows that we know about Rizzo while he has every reason to believe that we don't have a clue about Riverton!"

"Maybe we ought to alert the local deputy that we may be headed his way," I said, "although getting him into this wouldn't be doing him any favors!"

"Would you say that he was G.I.?" McLeod asked.

"Very much so!" I said.

"If you have his number call him," McLeod said. "We can use every man we can get. Maybe our advantage will be enough to discourage Kroll from wanting to shoot it out!"

I got hold of Jason and gave him the story. "Marked unit or plain?" he asked without hesitation.

"Marked unit or plain?" I repeated aloud.

"Marked!" McLeod said without hesitation. "And have him wait for our call!"

"Are you going to be in charge of this escapade?" Evans asked McLeod.

"I am in charge of everything up to the arrest!" McLeod said. "After the arrest we will defer to you! Everyone okay with that?"

We all murmured our agreement!

The rain had stopped but it still looked cold outside the purring, heated automobile. We passed Jacob Lake but it wasn't until we began to reach the outer limits of Fredonia that Riverton's car started to slow. It finally left the highway on the near side of town.

A couple of minutes later we passed the spot. There was a modest house set well back from the road against a thicket of trees. Two cars sat in front, one of them the rental from Flagstaff, the other half-hidden. We went on down the road and found a spot to stop, turning around so we could watch the house in question.

"They are liable to leave in the stolen car," Evans said. "Did anyone get a good look at it?"

"It's the blue Camry that belonged to the late salesman," McLeod said.

"My guess is that they will be coming out in one car or the other any minute!" Evans said.

It took less than ten minutes for Bridges to arrive and we all got out in the cold to convene!

'The house is supposed to be empty!" Bridges told us. "The old man was moved into an assisted living facility and one of his grandson's is supposed to take up occupancy early next year. Kroll obviously knew that!"

"Did the old man have any heavy artillery?" I asked.

"He well could have! He was no slouch in his early years! But I really don't have any idea about that!"

"What's behind the house?" Donovan wanted to know.

"Heavy woods lead down to a river and on the other side is the Hammond Ranch. If he went out the back he would have a quarter of a mile of thicket in each direction! One thing is sure he is not going to take on the river on a night like this even though it is small!"

"If we get up there before they try to leave we ought to disable the cars first!" Evans said.

"Too risky!" McLeod said. "I would rather let Kroll try to reach the cars than us! Anyway, it's five against two and one of them can't be that well trained. Those are pretty good odds as far as I'm concerned!

"So here's the plan! We are going to give Kilbane and Evans fifteen minutes to work their way through the woods to positions at the rear of the house. Then Jim and I are going to take positions toward the front within the trees. Then we are going to have Jason drive his marked unit down the street and turn around so that the driver's side is away from the house and come back and put the nose inside the line of trees. We want Kroll to be able to see the marked unit. Then we will use the PA to offer him a fair chance to surrender and good luck with that idea!"

None of us really expected to take Kroll alive.

It was already dark and cold enough to numb the feet. Donovan drove to the edge of the woods where McLeod and I jumped out and I started winding my way through the trees alongside the property. Donovan then took Evans and himself down the road to the other side.

I snaked between the trees until I took up a position at the northwest corner of the house with about ten yards of trees between me and the clearing and about fifty yards of clearing to the house. I unsnapped the holster, and readied my gun but opted to keep my hands in my pockets to keep them from getting cold. It had begun to drizzle again and it was freezing!

In minutes we could hear McLeod's voice on the P.A. system. Given the option of Kroll coming out or us going in there wasn't much doubt about how that was going to play. Lights inside the house were still on but the shades were drawn. And everything remained quiet until, from our position in the backyard, we heard a door slam and a pleading voice that had to belong to Riverton.

"Don't shoot! Don't shoot! Please don't shoot!" came the cry.

Still silence. Then McLeod, on the microphone, ordered him to come forward. It was an unfortunate distraction but at the same time it left us with one less body to worry about.

And then it happened. So fast that it almost stunned me into a delayed reaction. Kroll burst out of my side of the house with an automatic rifle blazing. From a standing crouch he raked the woods back and forth at least twice. I burrowed into the ground behind a tree as the bullets flew! They were digging into the ground, some of them ricocheting just above my head and shoulders so close I could hear the whine and feel the heat. I was sure he couldn't see me but was merely clearing the area before he came running right at me.

He stopped waving his rifle around as he hit the trees and he was closing the distance between us. He was less than seven feet away when I came up in a crouch and started firing.

This son of a bitch would certainly have a vest, I thought! But I needed a target in the dark and it had to be the center of mass. With my eyes boring into his chest I squeezed them off. All five shots! If he was wearing a vest the impact nonetheless stopped him in his tracks and brought him down to his knees, leaning away and grappling for his fallen rifle.

Instinctively I gave the rifle a solid kick sending it flying end over end and bouncing off trees. I swung the gun hand with as much force as I could and caught him on the side of his face sending him reeling. In the next instant Evans arrived firing down on Kroll's head and shoulders and I took a few quick steps out of the way, emptying the cylinder and reloading as I went.

Tom stood there firing until a couple of clicks told him that his gun was empty. He dropped the magazine and replaced it and for a moment I really thought he was going to empty another clip. Instead he took aim for a second before finally holstering his weapon

I was reminded of the shooting of a brutal cop-killer in Polk County where officers had taken particular pains to ensure his passing. When asked why the suspect had been shot twenty-three times, Sheriff Grady Judd simply replied, "Because we ran out of ammunition!"

Our other three officers arrived to form a circle around the fallen Kroll who by then was crumpled into a fetal position. The side of his head looked like it was hit with a grenade. The blood seeping from the front of his shirt told me that he wasn't wearing a vest after all!

"Is anybody hurt?" McLeod asked in a manner reminiscent of my football coaches after a game.

Tom and I shook our heads while looking each other over. It was no small miracle when you consider that Kroll had tossed off enough lead to pin down a battalion.

"That is your basic SIG Sauer 516!" Donovan said, eyeing the fallen weapon. "I wonder if it was his!"

"Knowing him, he probably had it stashed somewhere in case he got into trouble." I said. "He was the kind of guy who was always thinking ahead! Did anyone check to see if he had an automatic gun license?"

"I guess you can't think of everything!" McLeod said dryly.

"We're going to need a forensics unit," Donovan said. "And we won't be able to get a chopper out of Flagstaff tonight!"

"We can bring one from Las Vegas," Evans said.

"We can call on Kane County," Jason said. "They're right up the road!"

"That's even better!" Evans said. "Get them on the horn!" The authority had now passed seamlessly to the senior agent.

"What about our friend in the patrol car?" McLeod asked, suddenly remembering. "What are we going to do about him, assuming that he hasn't kicked out a window and taken off by now!"

"Let him go!" Tom said. "He didn't get his chance to help Kroll and, in fact, he did us a favor by leading us to him! So let him go!"

Bridges started off toward the car when Evans stopped him. "Do you have any plastic gloves in the car? We really ought to go through the formality of checking his pulse in all that goo!"

"If he's not dead he's doing a very good impression," Donovan said. "In fact he reminds me that I really need to screen in my patio!"

Even within sight of the fallen Kroll we were able to laugh. There was relief in the laughter, too. We'd been shot at and survived. In just over two months from the day I climbed the stairs to the wrap-around deck of the town house in Hillsboro the hunt for Caroline's killer had come to an end. I thought about Stoddard Lee, and Margaret and even Bear! Like Kroll said there was no bringing the beautiful Caroline back but this was the best we could do!